"We write to taste life twice,
in the moment and in retrospection."
~ *Anaïs Nin*

The human experience, however, is universal and I have been moved, saddened and deeply inspired by other people's lives over and over, and have inevitably drawn on my feelings in relation to many people's journeys. For this, I give thanks.

Radio Birch

'And it's a beautiful morning over the valley. We're expecting a high of 28 degrees Celsius and clear blue skies,' the familiar, gravelly voice promised over the kitchen radio. 'Today we're asking: Is it true that life really begins at forty, or does it all go downhill from there? This is a competition with a difference. There's no right or wrong answer! We're looking for the most convincing reply. The winner will go on a mystery lunch date, courtesy of this station. Phone Radio Birch now...'

The haunting strains of Janis Ian's *At Seventeen* replaced the warm tones of the breakfast radio announcer.

'Does life begin at forty? I sometimes wonder if part of my life was over a long time ago,' Topaz moaned to herself.

'What rubbish!' Sapphire scolded from her wooden settle by the Aga. Placing her tea down, she slowly walked to Topaz. Looking her older sister right in the eye, she said firmly, 'You're strong and capable. You had a glitch. A wrinkle. Yes, it damn well hurt, I'm not saying otherwise, but you'll learn to love again. It's nothing to do with age. You just need to let your heart open. Melt a little. Sis, your life hasn't even started.' With that, Sapphire coolly walked to the phone, dialled, and asked to speak to Josh Landing.

Mortified, Topaz ran into the garden as soon as she realised what her little sister was up to. 'There's no-one out there for me', she muttered to the air, but almost as soon as the words escaped her lips there was something in the tunes of the morning birdsong that told her differently. She felt exposed and embarrassed, as if every living entity in the garden stopped its business to look at her. The exquisitely scented honeysuckle, intent on covering the rusty garden shed in a symbiotic dance, shot its heady fragrance her way as if to say, 'Here, dab some of this on your wrist young lady.'

The red squirrel, a daily visitor to their rambling English country garden, looked up from the nut feeder and hinted that it was an abundant life: 'Plenty for everyone.'

'Shut up,' she impatiently told the voice in her head, for fear she was going crazy.

And the morning Sun had a thing or two to say as well. Who knew it could be this warm in Britain at 7am? Warming her frozen heart, perhaps?

'Topes, breakfast is ready.' Mischievous to the core, Sapphire's melodic voice beckoned her love-worn sister back indoors. Topaz deliberately stopped by the strawberries and waited for a few moments as she sucked on their juices. 'Gifts. They're gifts,' the voice inside told her as she made her way to the kitchen.

Sapphire couldn't contain herself, bubbling with excitement. 'Today's a good day. It's going to be a good day. I can feel it!' They both jumped as the phone cut through Sapphire's declarations. 'You get it,' she motioned to Topaz. 'It'll be for you.'

Topaz frowned, her eyebrows knitting together defiantly. *No,* she thought. *No, not the darn radio station. I don't need this.*

'Good morning. Topaz Lane speaking.'

'Good morning Topaz, Josh Landing, Radio Birch. Congratulations! You're live on the air at Radio Birch, and the winner of our Does Life Begin at 40? Mystery Lunch Date.'

Her heart sank. Colour flooded her cheeks. Decades of sister love was not enough to get Sapphire free from the evil-eyed glare of Topaz. Like a rabbit in headlights, Topaz didn't know where to look or what to say.

'Topaz, are you there?' the deep voice asked down the line, inviting her up for air.

'Er, um.'

'Topaz, you've won a mystery lunch. Stay on the line and we'll give you details of the big day. Do get in touch afterwards so we can let our listeners know how you went, and if it's true that life really does begin at forty.'

'OH MY GOD. Topaz, you're going on a date!' Sapphire couldn't contain her excitement any longer, bouncing up and down on the spot.

'Shut up, Saph!' Topaz ordered without remorse. 'I can't believe you'd pretend you were me.' She stormed out of the kitchen without eating her breakfast. 'I'm going to work!'

They rarely fell out, and when they did the pain of separation and hurt always had them readily able to forgive. *This was different*, Topaz justified to herself. Her fingers traced the mint and fennel as she moved towards her garden-based art studio. Inside the wooden chalet, she grabbed an HB pencil and began to outline a sketch.

For sixteen years Topaz Lane had enjoyed a passionate career as a children's illustrator, and was highly sought after by some of the biggest publishing houses in the world. At heart, she was a private girl, and that's why she shunned the limelight. She enjoyed the solitude of working from home. And now she was going on a blind date. What was Sapphire thinking?

She didn't dare turn on the radio. They'd be blowing her name on the airwaves all day long. Instead, she played Mozart. Good old Mozart. Faithful, reliable Mozart. Always there for her, Mozart. Honest Mozart. Mozart for inspiration; Mozart for solace. And as those words ran through her head she began to whimper, then sob. How could Topaz ever love again? *That would be impossible*, she'd told herself many times. Her life was dedicated to children's art and… to the children she'd never have. And she kept crying. Grief respected no boundaries. He was relentless, and pushed, pushed, pushed. Grief always asked 'Who are you? How deep do you go? Where's the real you? Come on, I dare you to…*feel*.'

How can this still hurt so much? Why can't I let go? she asked herself over and over.

Most of her day was spent curled up on the studio sofa, reliving the agony of the years gone by. Raw, aching, and never-ending.

A tap came at the glass French doors at 8pm. 'Topaz, I know you're furious, but you need to eat. You've worked for twelve hours straight, love. Come and have your dinner. Please.'

Topaz didn't say that she'd hardly worked, but instead had cried for twelve hours. A whole work day spent reliving the ache, pain, hurt, betrayal and loss. But Sapphire could see for herself that there'd been a whole lot of crying. She turned off the CD player and put Mozart to sleep. She acknowledged Topaz by raising her eyebrows. Together they walked, hand in hand, along the long and winding garden path to the converted barn they shared.

The evening Summer Sun wrapped itself across their bodies like a luminous garland. 'I'm so sorry

Topes. I thought I was helping. I really am sorry. I hope you can forgive me.'

Topaz didn't reply, but grabbed a knife and fork from the wicker cutlery tray. But just as she was about to sit at the old wooden farmhouse kitchen table, her heart stopped as she spied a cream-coloured envelope with her name on it. Handwritten: *Topaz Lane;* in the top corner of the envelope, the words *Radio Birch*, and their county-wide familiar silver birch logo.

'I'm sorry, sis. It was hand delivered with those roses,' Sapphire motioned toward the old pine dresser at the far end of the kitchen. Inside a tall vase were 40 ruby roses. Topaz ate her meal of roast red peppers stuffed with spicy quinoa: her eyes never leaving the envelope. She was used to seeing her name in print; inside children's books, outside children's books; on press releases, promotional posters. *This was different.* She had no control over this. She hadn't agreed to this!

'I'll open it then!' Sapphire said, infuriated, ripping it apart.

Dear Topaz, re: Does Life Begin at Forty? To celebrate your 34th birthday, you'll be dining at McVickery's Watermill, all expenses paid. July 3rd. Best wishes, Josh Landing and the team at Radio Birch.

July 2nd: Another work day wasted. Deadline looming. But all Topaz could do was sit in the garden taking in the birdsong, and little else. Her bare feet imprinted on the chamomile lawn as she stretched back into the bench. Who was she having lunch with tomorrow? A celebrity? A man? Oh my God, a blind date? She felt sick to her stomach. She hadn't been on a date since Andy, and she met him more than 15 years ago, when she was little more than a girl out of college. *I can't do this,* she pleaded aloud to the flowers.

'Oh yes you can!' piped Sapphire's voice from beyond the honeysuckle. 'You can, and you will. It's just lunch. It's not a marriage vow. It's just lunch. Relax.'

'If it's so darn relaxing, why don't you go on the date?' Topaz demanded, even though she knew there was no point as Sapphire was in a happy long-term relationship.

'Simple, really. It's not my birthday tomorrow, and I don't believe my love life has ended. I'm not walking around like a 16-year-old war widow.' The harshness of her words shut them both up.

Topaz woke long before the morning Sun pierced its light into her bedroom. She admired the Dufton red sandstone which surrounded the window, and how it shimmered like miniature crystals in the light. Had she even been asleep? The honeysuckle wafted through the window, reminding her: *Here, dab a bit of this on. Dress like a lady. Have fun.*

Happy birthday, she muttered to her sleepy self in the mirror. No butterflies flew in the garden this morning. They were all at war in her belly. Her sister was nowhere to be seen. No note, no gifts. Surely she'd not forgotten? By noon, Topaz had outlined a few sketches and felt satisfied.

McVickery's Watermill

The limo, arranged by Radio Birch, picked her up and delivered her to the restaurant. She'd eaten there a number of times, and was delighted that it was chosen by the station. It was the envy of all the chefs in town, boasting the finest gourmet foods. Reservations were usually made months in advance.

Topaz stood at reception, quickly glancing across the open courtyard. McVickery's Watermill was nestled against a strong flowing beck, the waterwheel providing much electricity for the restaurant. She couldn't see anyone dining alone. Maybe the celebrity date had changed his mind. All this anxiety for nothing! She'd been stood up! Darn.

'Miss Lane?' a young voice asked from behind the counter at reception.

'Yes. I've been stood up, haven't I?' she laughed nervously, and realised how incredibly disappointed she felt. *Men!*

'You're here as a guest of Radio Birch? Your dining companions are this way.'

Companions? Topaz thought it must have been a grammatical error. She was led to a table of what sounded like a bunch of cackling hens. Five women, deeply engaged in conversation and laughter, looked up when the young receptionist arrived and interrupted them.

'Excuse me ladies, your lunch guest is here. This is Topaz Lane. Shall I let you introduce yourselves?' The young waitress smiled, and then bowed away from the tableau of festivity. One by one they stood up and introduced themselves.

Topaz laughed out loud. 'I'm so sorry. I was

under the impression I was on a blind date with a celebrity. But I don't recognise any of you. Should I?' And with that, everyone laughed. 'Not a celebrity among us,' hooted Kate, an archaeologist in her mid fifties.

'Hi, I'm Kate. Happy Birthday! I think I've seen you before. Down at the farmers' market on a Saturday morning?'

Topaz relaxed a little. 'Yes, that's right. I pick up my fruit and vegetables from there,' she said, trying to calm her nerves. 'I have to say this is the most unusual birthday I've ever had. My sister put me up for this competition. I was dead against it. Does life begin at forty? What would I know? I'm 34.'

Kate laughed. 'The forties are great, but the fifties are even better. You really come into your own. It's as if you find that your skin really does fit you, and, well, for me, this is the best time of my life. I'm sure of who I am. Other people's opinions of me don't matter or bother me. I'm true to myself in a way that I wasn't thirty or forty years ago.' Kate was a striking-looking woman with spiky salt-and-pepper-shaded hair, wrapped in a twirled purple headscarf which matched her unusual lilac earrings. They were made from small tiles. 'Sit down, Topaz,' she said, pulling a velvet padded chair out for her.

'Hi Topaz, I'm Annie. It's such an honour to be here sharing your birthday. I'm 22, and mother to five-year-old Zac. Most of the time I feel like I'm forty! Or eighty. Becoming a mum when I was 17 woke me up really quickly, and I've lived so much in this last half decade that I can't even imagine how much more full or rich life could be in my forties. Zac will have left home by then. I'm not sure who I'll be when I'm not being a mother. Anyway, happy birthday!'

14

Topaz could feel her eyes welling up with tears. If there was any gift she could have for her birthday, it would be a child. And here was this woman before her, no more than a child herself, living her greatest wish. The irony! *Happy birthday?* she thought to herself. Whoever thought to bring along this young mother to celebrate her birthday couldn't have known what a cruel attempt at festivity it was. She smiled meekly, trying to keep back the tears.

Róisín sensed something amiss, and smiled assuredly at Topaz. When she felt that their eyes were fully engaged, she introduced herself. 'My name is spelled R.O.I.S.I.N, but pronounced Ro SHEEN. Hey, happy solar return, Topaz. I remember my 34th birthday well.' The lyrically spoken Irish woman tilted back her head; silver plaits flicked over her shoulders. 'I'd just completed my apprenticeship as a midwife. I'm 66 now, and have no intention of retiring. I love what I do. I hope the years which lay ahead bring you as much joy, inspiration and wisdom as my life has brought me. Does life begins at 40? It begins any time we give ourselves permission to live fully and freely without apology. There's definitely a change in spirit, courage and consciousness that hits when we're about forty, though it's usually preceded by confusion, doubt and lots of mayhem! When we break through, especially our fear of mortality, then the great shift happens. We wake and smell the coffee, and really get stuck into living. The producer at Radio Birch asked each of us to bring you a gift that didn't cost us anything. I'd like to gift you with something from my life, but we can talk about that later,' she promised.

'I'm Francesca, and this is Lia.' Francesca reached out both of her hands and took Topaz's hands into her own. Topaz could feel that her fingers were rough like sandpaper, and observed that her skin was golden brown. She figured hers must be an outside job. 'Thanks for coming today, Francesca and Lia.'

Topaz was starting to feel uncomfortable, which struck her as odd since each of these women was so warm and inviting. She realised she was completely out of her comfort zone being amongst all these strangers.

'What inspired you to come today?'

Lia answered immediately. She had short, blonde, silky hair cut into a crop, and a smattering of freckles. 'I'm a writer, and I simply love to watch humans interact. I sit for hours in cafés observing people. The idea of life not beginning until we're forty strikes me as utterly ridiculous. I've been writing solidly for about twenty years and I can't imagine what could possibly happen in five years from now that will make me feel like I've been dead all this time! I've travelled the world, stayed in great cities, slow-danced to jazz saxophone in New Orleans, taught reading in an orphanage in Russia, cycled across Holland, trekked the Rockies, picked tea in India, and ridden elephants in South Africa.

In one year alone I backpacked across Australia, picked gala apples on an orchard in Hawke's Bay, New Zealand; snorkelled off the coast of Fiji; took a life-drawing class in New York city, and volunteered in a soup kitchen for the homeless. I've lived. I'm living. My gift to you is this blank notebook,' she said proudly, pulling a bound book from her handbag. 'I've found that writing down five things each day that I'm grateful for has brought so much to my life. It's an honour to be alive. I hope you'll take this in the spirit in which it's given, and keep a daily gratitude journal.

I hope that life has already begun for you.' And with that, Lia handed over the book as if she were handing her most precious possession to Topaz. 'Enjoy,' she whispered, and gave a wink of support.

Something jolted within Topaz. Perhaps it was recognition that she'd spent so much time lately being ungrateful; so much time looking at the glass half-empty rather than looking at the abundance of love, joy, happiness and creativity that abounded in her life. She was leaving a legacy of art to millions of people, and yet all she could do, day in and day out, was to feel sorry for herself about an incident which happened years before. So many people would swap their lives with hers in a heartbeat.

Francesca had hair the colour of marmalade, which hung in huge ringlets over her shoulders. She passed a small, brown, unmarked packet over to Topaz. 'These are seeds: a mixture of wildflower seeds. I'm a gardener, and felt that the gift I wanted to share with you was something connected to life. I can tell you what flowers are likely to come up from this batch of seeds, but I'd rather it was a surprise. Like life! We can plot and plan and try and control the outcome of everything, but often it's the unexpected that brings the most rewards, even if they initially seem painful. Trust that the seeds we plant today will emerge strong and vibrant when the time is right.' Francesca reached into her purse for a photograph. 'This was me three years ago, at 40. I owned a florist at the top end of town.'

'Yes, I know it!' Topaz exclaimed. 'Sunflower Express?'

'Yes. I'd been arranging flowers for about twenty five years. I went into the business when I was quite young, and really loved it. I honestly did. But one day

17

I woke up and thought: *I want to grow flowers not deal with ones that are in the process of dying*. I sold the shop, and although it was sad to leave behind the clientele I'd built up, I've never been happier than now, with my hands in the soil and the Sun on my skin. I still get excited with each new seedling that emerges. It feels like the greatest miracle on Earth. I never take it for granted. My friends thought I was having a mid-life crisis. Maybe I was!' she laughed. 'But I knew I had to do it. Life's too short not to follow our dreams. I hope you'll follow yours.'

The waitress arrived to take their orders: Wild mushrooms, dill and roasted garlic in filo pastry; marinated artichoke, pesto and olive sourdough pizza; caramelised red onion tart; pumpkin and spinach lasagna; lentil rissoles in red-pepper sauce; chilli bean stew and nachos. The women shared a selection of seasonal salads, and crisp white wine. 'Oh my, this is good!' Topaz declared, savouring every mouthful of the sweet onion tart.

'You should try this pizza! I adore artichokes,' Kate said, licking her fingers, and offering a mouthful of pizza to the others. Then they all took turns at sharing their meals. The women oooed and aaahed, taking samples here and there. Foodgasms of appreciation abounded. The afternoon ambled along on coffee and cake, with much laughter and the forging of friendships.

'Topaz, you're probably wondering why I haven't given you a gift yet. Like Róisín, I wanted to share my work with you. I'm an archaeologist,' said Kate, 'and I wondered if you fancy coming along on a dig?'

Nodding approvingly, she answered without hesitation. 'That sounds fun. Thank you!'

'My other little gift will be given to you then,' Kate hinted, with her trademark twinkling eyes. *She makes women in their fifties look like Goddesses*, Topaz noted. Her beauty and grace was something to be admired.

As the late afternoon Sun sank towards the skyline, the women reluctantly grabbed their bags and left the mill. None of them wanted to break up the party. Something had touched each of them that day; something that reminded them that life is what we make it.

'Hey, why should we break this up now? Why don't we head back to my place and sit under the stars for a while?' suggested Kate. It was unanimous. They shared cars, and drove to her home at the edge of the lake. The evening was stunning. The stars above were silent witnesses to the women's lives.

Gathering themselves comfortably onto rugs and cushions Kate had brought down from the house, they poured tea from a Thermos, and together they built a small fire from old logs and branches that had been swept up on the pebbled shoreline of the lake.

'We don't know much about you, Topaz,' Róisín stated, looking directly into her eyes, and smiling warmly. 'We've told you heaps about us and our lives. Why don't you share a bit with us?'

Topaz was taken by surprise. She added some twigs to the lively, crackling fire, and focused intently on the flames. Topaz hoped they'd be distracted by the crackling and popping, but no such luck. She felt five sets of eyes on her. *Oh God.*

'Not much to say. Average life. No husband, no children. Great career. Lovely sister and parents. A beautiful home and garden. Fabulous career, actually. I love it! That's it, really. Sorry to disappoint,' she grimaced, sketching lines into the sand and pebbles with her safety-blanket stick.

'Everyone has a story, Topaz,' Kate coaxed. 'Tell us about your career. How did you get started?'

She felt a bit safer in this territory. No digging about long-lost loves and other pain. 'I went to Fine Art school and specialised in children's illustration. I submitted some pieces to a publishing house, just on spec, really. I never expected anything to come from that. It was a college assignment. I received a phone call twenty-four hours later with a commission offer! I dropped out of college within weeks because I had too much work on my plate. And the work has rolled in ever since. It's been amazing, really. It's as if someone sprinkled gold dust on that part of my life. I've been able to travel, and enjoy all sorts of adventures and experiences, and to meet authors...'

'But?' Róisín queried.

'But? There's no but. It's been fantastic. My career is still fantastic. I love every working day. I've made such a name for myself that I can pick and choose without ever having to compromise my integrity,' Topaz insisted. 'And I have the luxury of working from home. No commuting! I live with my sister, Sapphire, who teaches cello.'

Róisín kept digging. 'It feels like there's something you're not telling us. You don't have to, of course; but you know, you're in safe company here. No-one's going to judge you.' And with that, it was as if someone had put their arms firmly around Topaz, and in a weak moment she felt herself flooded in tears.

'Please, don't. This is my *birthday*. Let's keep things the way they were. It's been such a fabulous day. I don't want to ruin things,' she pleaded.

Kate joined in. She could see where Róisín was

heading. 'There's no shame in digging deep, Topaz. It makes our lives richer. The more we hide and suppress the less likeable parts of ourselves or our lives the more they sabotage the good in our lives. Everyone has a wound of some sort. We're only ever as strong or as happy as our weakest points. Has there been a man?'

'Of course there's been a *man*!' retorted Topaz. 'But do we really have to bring *him* to my birthday?'

'Can't you see he's here anyway? He's behind everything you say and do. Every hesitation. Unless you can let him go, then he'll always tag along,' Lia offered. 'What happened, Topaz?' she asked kindly.

'Andy slept with my best friend. I was three months pregnant.' Topaz couldn't keep the pain in any longer. Francesca's arms were around her. 'Let it out, girl. Let it out.'

Annie added, 'I thought you didn't have children.'

Topaz shook her head from side to side. Her sobs kept catching in her throat. Speaking was an impossibility. The floodgates opened. What had they started with all their questioning? The women took turns in adding twigs and small branches to the fire, keeping alight that mystical sacred space, instinctively knowing the healing power of fire to burn away negativity.

It was a long time before Topaz could catch her breath and speak; then when she did, her words left her new friends in no doubt of the pain which shadowed her young life and influenced her decision to decline dates. Róisín spoke a few wise words, hoping to illicit a response: *the wound reveals the cure*. Topaz looked a little puzzled. 'I met Andy just after college. He was the love of my life.'

'Darling, the love of your life doesn't sleep with someone else. Ever...' Kate assured her.

Róisín agreed. 'You were gestating your love child, and he was making merry elsewhere. Of course that hurts!'

'All I ever wanted was a baby. A family. A home. *A nest*. Yes, it's great making art for children. I love being with children, and signing books in bookshops: but I wanted my own children. I went to Cassie's house because she'd cancelled a movie date due to a bad cold. I made up a batch of home-made soup, hoping it would cheer her up. She loved my soup. You see, we were best friends since kindergarten. We knew everything about each other, or so I thought. Obviously *not* everything.

I had a key to her flat. To see my husband in bed, with her: my best friend, naked, doing what he did with me, killed something inside me. I lost faith in life, in love. I lost faith in me; in who I was. It was as if someone had cut my heart out. The grief consumed me, and I lost the baby.

I was a mum-to-be, and was so proud. I'd already painted the nursery in fairy-tale characters: a good use of my talents, ironically; but I couldn't hold onto that baby no matter how much I wanted. The part of me that I shared with Andy just disintegrated in my body. The bleeding went on and on, as if my body wasn't ever going to let go.'

Topaz stopped for a moment, almost as if she was speaking about someone else. For the first time, she felt distanced from the memory. Perhaps it was the act of verbalising all those years of deeply held pain. Something had released within her; been freed, like a caged bird finally given an open door.

Measuring each word for accuracy, without the

attachment of emotion, she continued, 'Andy was shocked that he'd been discovered. Apparently they'd been having an affair since before we were married. Finally he could be honest with me. I could never understand why he stayed with me; why he married me when he was clearly in love with her. Maybe he felt sorry for me. Maybe he was just a coward. It's strange to be here, on a shoreline. Maybe that's why I feel so fragile, so vulnerable. We held our baby's farewell ceremony on a beach. Hearing these waves, as we sit here tonight, gently lapping on the shore... brings it all back. It was in Summer. I've always loved the way I feel when I'm near water.

Although I couldn't stand the sight of Andy, I'm grateful, in a strange way, that he was part of that goodbye ceremony. It would have been the last straw if he'd denied his fatherhood. I expect he still feels guilty for how it all turned out. He was a mess, too, yet he couldn't share his feelings with me about our baby's death. We wrote her name in shells on the beach: GRACE. I lit candles, and placed coastal wildflowers all around. We sang, strummed guitar, and played that song: *Everybody Hurts Some Time*.

There was magic in the madness of those crazy, blurred-together days, and yet the enormity of what happened closed me down. I could feel it. I knew what was happening, yet felt powerless to stop its hold on me; on my heart.'

Topaz looked around the small circle of women. 'I thought I was meeting celebrities today, but you're just ordinary people like me. Kind, ordinary women with *extraordinary* hearts. Thank you for holding me within this space. I feel that I've made five new friends today. I've probably passed you on the streets many times, and yet it's only now we've connected; only now that our lives have touched. I wonder why that is? Were we destined to meet?'

Each of the women had tears in her eyes.

Overwhelmed with emotion, no-one could speak for some time until Kate, in her usual comical manner, piped up. 'I know just the man for you!' They all laughed, even Topaz. 'Seriously, Kate. What man wants to end up with a mop bucket of emotions like me?'

'Not all men are created equal, you know,' winked Lia. And all the women burst into hysterical laughter. 'I didn't mean it like *that*! Hey, let's have a dinner party and each bring along an eligible man. Sort of a blind-date dinner party...with all the men there for Topaz.'

'NOOOOOOOO!' shrieked Topaz, laughing and crying at such a preposterous idea.

'How totally brilliant,' shot Annie into the circle. 'My dad would be perfect. He's been alone for most of my life. He's amazing. I'd not have survived parenting if it wasn't for him. He's my rock. I know he probably sounds old because he's a grandad, but he's not! Honest!'

'My husband's best friend is *really* hot. I reckon you'd like him,' added Lia.

'And my cousin hasn't dated in ages, I'll invite him along,' said Kate, throwing his name into the mix.

'I don't like where this is going,' said Topaz, shaking her head from side to side, grinning all the while.

'No, this is great, Topaz. Honestly, it will be perfect. A big dinner party with none of the men knowing what's going on. It'll be great,' Kate laughed.

'My son's always up for a home-cooked meal.' Róisín was taking this seriously. 'You and he would be wonderful together, but he's not available. I'll ask my neighbour. He's quite charming.'

'I've got a seed supplier who is very easy on the eye. I reckon I could get him along to a dinner date,' smiled Francesca, who had quickly warmed to the plan.

'A seed supplier?' Kate roared, her laughter spreading contagiously round the circle.

'Seed supplier,' chuckled Lia, slapping her knees. Annie suppressed a giggle.

'Fabulous. This is fabulous. We'll heal that broken heart of yours Topaz. We'll put you back together again. You just wait and see!' promised Kate.

The Moon shimmied across the sky, and at half-past midnight the women made their way back to the cars, agreeing to meet for the dinner party. They swapped phone numbers. Annie said she'd call and arrange her gift. Lia drove Topaz home. As they made their way down the country lane towards the old converted barn, Lia said 'You'll be okay, Topaz. Something really big happened to you tonight. There was a palpable shift for you. I felt it, and so did the others.' They bade each other good night, and Topaz tiptoed up the path.

Sapphire had left the kitchen light on for her. Opening the door slowly, she slid inside inaudibly so as not to waken her. 'Where have you been?' snapped Sapphire, who was sitting in the corner of the kitchen. 'I've been beside myself with worry!'

Topaz jumped out of her skin. 'On the lunch date that YOU set up. It just went for longer than I expected.'

Sapphire's fury rapidly transformed to relief, and she proffered a gift. 'Happy birthday, Sis.'

Topaz looked quizzically at the envelope, and ripped it open. Inside was a voucher for a season of Salsa dance classes, and a pair of tickets to see her favourite singer. Topaz laughed. 'How perfect! This will be great for brightening up the dark Autumn evenings. Thanks so much. I'm sorry you were worried. I should have called. You weren't around this morning. Where were you, by the way?'

'Buying ingredients for *dinner,*' she smiled, pointing to the meal sitting on the stove. 'Oh, Saph!'

'Don't worry, we can have it for lunch tomorrow. Anyway, tell me about your date. Who was he? Was he famous?' she quizzed.

The sisters sipped tea by candlelight, and Topaz continued to let go of some of the deep hurt that had frozen, vice-like, around her tender heart. They both giggled like schoolgirls at the dinner party being planned. 'Hey, why don't you come, Saph? Bring Jeff. It'll be fun.'

Sapphire thought the whole scheme was brilliant, and suggested they held it at their home as it was spacious and well away from neighbours.

Topaz lay awake for hours that night. Thirty four, and love wasn't over for her. Could that really be true? What were the odds of one of the five men at the upcoming dinner party being a good match? *A good match,* she wondered. What did that mean? Would she choose more wisely than she did with Andy? Is there ever a way of knowing if a man can be faithful, honest, devoted, enduring? *Life isn't that safe,* she told herself. *And love certainly isn't! The only person I can trust to be faithful and honest is myself.* She pondered the truth for some time before slowly drifting off to sleep.

The Dig

Kate was the first woman to call Topaz. 'Hey, we've got a dig on Saturday. Are you up for it? It's down at Grizler's Flats. We'll take a picnic lunch,' she said, excitedly.

'Of course I'm up for it. I can't wait,' Topaz replied.

'Wear comfy shoes, I'll pick you up at eight. See ya,' Kate chirped down the phone.

Bright and early on Saturday morning, Kate threw her copy of *The Archaeologist's Handbook* into her backpack, dressed in khaki trousers and t-shirt, and headed off to Topaz's home. At 55, Kate was, by any beholder's opinion, a striking-looking, dynamic and vibrant woman. She made any room light up with her warm presence. Today she wore her silver-specked hair wrapped in a mesh, red headscarf which matched her unusual red earrings. They were made from small red tiles to form a mosaic.

'I love your earrings!' Topaz remarked when she slid into the passenger seat. 'They're amazing.'

'I'm glad you like them,' Kate smiled, and handed her a little packet. 'These are for you; they're part of your birthday present.'

'Really?' she asked, eagerly opening the black velvet pouch to find a pair of mosaic earrings. They were dark green, and matched her eyes. 'These are wonderful! Thank you so much.'

'They're to remind you of what you'll learn today. An archaeological dig is such an incredible metaphor for life. '

27

They drove for about half an hour, and Kate explained that the earliest-known mosaics were found at a temple building in Mesopotamia. Historians dated them to about the second half of the third millennium BC.

'Generally the pieces are of ivory, shells and coloured stones,' she explained.

Her passion for archaeology was contagious. 'Excavations from around 1500 BC showed evidence of the first glazed tiles. Mosaic patterns weren't used until the times of the Sassanid Empire, and were strongly influenced by the Romans.'

'So what's the metaphor, Kate?' Topaz asked curiously.

'Archaeology is the attempt to understand life by looking at the past. Personally, I've done a lot of looking at my past so that I could stand strong now.' She hesitated before continuing. 'I consider the soul to be a sacred site. Excavation, I can tell you, isn't always pleasant, or easy! You see, we often work in harsh conditions, the weather can be absolutely vile, and it requires painstaking effort....but all of that is worth it for the discovery. I wear the mosaic earrings as a reminder of what can be found when you go digging deep,' she hinted. 'The same idea applies to emotional and psychological excavations. The central tenet of my archaeological life is to search for small things. And if we apply it to life we end up living a meaningful and conscious, hand-crafted life. If we don't, then we end up living other people's lives by making unconscious choices.'

When they arrived at the site, Topaz discovered that Kate was the expedition director, and she was leading a team of teenagers from the local care home.

The kids scrambled off the bus, and put their bags under a tree. Kate hadn't mentioned that she was working with troubled teenagers, and Topaz was struck by her fine balance of humility and passion. Kate marked out the excavation site, and prepared the area for digging. She explained to Topaz that the topography ~ the surface appearance ~ acted as a reference point during the dig.

'A dig like this rests on observation, description and explanation; and that's what I hope to nurture in these teenagers,' Kate said, as if it were common sense.

Topaz joined Kate in putting her hands into the soil and carefully chipped away at fragments of sandstone. She wondered what they might find, if anything. At least with art, you could quickly see progress: a line or brushstroke on a page; something, *anything*! This was glacially slow.

'You can't rush an excavation,' Kate whispered. Topaz wondered if she'd actually said her thoughts out loud, and quickly became aware that her face flushed crimson. She felt embarrassed that she was so quick to judge this, and wondered if she should view it instead as an art form.

'If you hit hard rock, it can stop you in your tracks. The most important trait as an archaeologist is persistence. Other things are important, too, such as observation, curiosity and following your instinct. What I hope these kids will learn is that as you dig past the soil and rocks, you're also digging past your own expectations,' she said, moist beads of perspiration trickling down her tanned cheeks. 'Most of these kids have never had anyone expect anything from them. As we dig here, we're searching for things that have been forgotten. The physical act of doing this will ignite an emotional excavation for them. It will bring things to the surface that have been hidden for a very long time.' Kate smiled, sat back on her haunches, and shared a secret. 'I have a ninety per-cent success rate with getting these kids back living in mainstream society and not reoffending. Well, it's not me as such. It's the dig.'

'Really? Oh Kate, that's incredible!' Topaz almost reached over to hug her. She was learning more and more about what a unique and incredible human being Kate was, and felt gratitude that they were becoming friends.

Kate had no children of her own, but had already shared that she didn't have a deep urge to become a mother herself. Topaz could see that these teenagers were her children, even though they were only with Kate for short periods of time. These young humans felt the depths of her passion and love.

'Why did you become an archaeologist, Kate?' Topaz asked.

'Do you want the long story or the short one?' Kate replied, hands back in the soil.

Picking up the Pieces

Kate, aged eleven

The wiry, prepubescent brown-haired girl gingerly picked up the crumpled local newspaper that her distraught mother had dropped on the kitchen floor before escaping from the room. Surveying the front page, Kate wiped the tears from her eyes, and read:

Popular Rotary man arrested on sexual-abuse charges

The local community has been shocked that a leading figure has been charged on seventeen counts of sexual abuse against minors.

Kevin Henry, aged 45, had been instrumental in setting up the town's community youth centre, and volunteered part-time at many youth events.

Locals say that they would never have suspected that such a well-known figure could be capable of these charges.

Kate saw her name and her mother's name in print, and she too dropped the contaminated item. In anger, she picked it up again and burnt the newspaper in the fireplace. She was still reeling from the shock that the man whose lap she sat on every night for cuddles was the monster that the town claimed him to be, and now she was being mentioned in the same article, as if their relationship somehow implicated her! Why did she have to be identified? 'I'm nothing like him!' she yelled out the front door, and then slammed it shut. She ran to her bedroom, crying.

Eventually, her mother came in to comfort her, but in truth she needed comfort, too. Their world had just been torn apart from left field without hint or warning. Not only were they losing their husband and father to a prison cell, they would have to adjust to life in the public eye as 'tainted people'.

'The only way we can survive this, Kit Kat,' she sniffed, 'is if we move far away where no-one knows us. Then, and only then, can we start again,' her mother said, tears soaking her long-sleeved t-shirt. 'I'm so sorry. I just can't see any other way.'

'But my friends? My school? My geography group? I can't leave all that behind. It's not fair. I didn't do anything wrong!' she screamed, then sobbed into the soft pillow, her feet kicking the bed like a raging toddler.

After a few minutes, when the feet-drumming subsided, her mother acknowledged her innocence. 'I know you didn't my love, but I know what people are like. They won't forget this. It will be a poisonous cloud that hangs over our heads for years to come. If we go where we're not known, at least there's a chance for the Sun to shine in our lives.' She touched the cheek of her daughter's red, blotchy face, wiping the tears. 'You deserve better than to be shamed by him.'

Within two days, Kate and her mother left their Southern suburban life, and moved north to the outskirts of a small Cumbrian market town, three hundred miles away from the shame. Kate was reluctant to make friends and to create a new life. She couldn't get her father's face out of her mind, and started to second-guess everything about the relationship they'd had. Did he ever abuse her, she wondered? Did it happen before she was old enough to realise? *But he was such a nice man to everyone*, she would often say to herself. It just didn't make sense.

Kate wrote letters to her father, pleading, begging, hoping that he might give her answers. Maybe there was a misunderstanding. Maybe the allegations were false. They had to be! Her mother never did let her attend the trial and hear from the witnesses. 'What if they were all lying?' Kate asked over and over again. She beseeched her father to come home by writing to him each day. In every spare moment, she studied the psychological profiles of paedophiles, trying to find answers, clues and resolution. She even had several sessions of hypnotherapy to see if he'd ever touched her inappropriately. He hadn't. *So why all those other girls and boys?* she wondered over and over again. These were rocky years for Kate, and she often felt herself drowning in the shame and pain. This was not what the teenage years were meant to look like.

At the end of high school, she attended a book launch held in her town. The author had written about his life as an archaeologist in the Middle East, even though he was only 27 years old. Their attraction was instant, despite the age difference. Sven befriended her, but waited until she was eighteen before asking her on a date. He introduced her to archaeology, often taking her on digs. In time, she confided to him about her father. Sharing such a profoundly dark and sordid secret bound them together. She found solace and relief from years of private pain.

Kate discovered therapy in archaeology; and together with Sven, led an annual overseas tour for troubled teenagers, exploring different digs.

Eventually, she set up digs in her area, working on behalf of the local care home for troubled teenagers. She had found her calling in life, and would be the first to admit that it almost certainly wouldn't have happened had her life not taken the disastrous turn that it had in her own pre-teenage years. Living for so long with an honest and kind person like Sven also renewed her faith in mankind, and in men.

The Shamanic Midwife

Topaz arrived at Róisín's home for 2pm. 'I've never thought much about home births before,' she mused as they drove the dusty road to the client's house a few miles from a small village. Róisín had invited Topaz to an antenatal appointment as a belated birthday present. She felt that it was a gift that would be unique.

'Andy's father was a doctor, so there was no question that they wanted the baby born in hospital.'

'I used to work in hospitals, but it's a very different experience. It wasn't me. Hospitals are a distraction for mother and midwife. Too many rules and protocols. Telling a woman how to give birth actually robs her of one of the greatest gifts of motherhood. Many hospital births have an element of intrusion about them, though most people don't see that; they just consider the practices to be normal. I quickly learnt that normal does not mean natural.'

Topaz was shocked by such a revelation, and then added, reflectively, 'You must really love babies to be a midwife,' Topaz offered.

'Babies?' Róisín laughed. 'A person doesn't become a midwife because they love babies; they do so because they love women. The baby is such a small part of the equation, even though the event is clearly about their arrival Earthside. It really is about women: caring for them emotionally, physically, mentally and spiritually. In a hospital setting, it tends to just be the physical side that's monitored.'

'Sounds to me that what you're doing is more of a way of life than a job.'

Róisín smiled, 'That's so true. I've changed enormously as a woman since I first began as a midwife.

35

I consider myself now to be a shamanic midwife, because I'm led from the heart. My midwifery kit is very simple: my healing hands, which I try to keep off the woman where possible. And of course, there's my word medicine: positive and affirmative words to lead the mother onwards to her birthing. Finally, I have faith in her ability to birth. Yes, it is a way of life, that's for sure. It's not something you turn off when you leave a client's house or birth.'

'The way you describe midwifery compared to shamanic midwifery sounds like chalk and cheese. How do you move from one to the other? What changed things around for you?' Topaz asked with great curiosity.

Róisín took a few moments to answer, unsure of how much to share with Topaz in light of the other evening around the lakeside fire.

'When I was eighteen, I gave birth to my first child, Eden. She was such a beautiful baby, but she ... only took a few breaths, and then died,' Róisín sighed.

Topaz gasped aloud. 'I'm so sorry.' Tears welled in her eyes. Was she crying for herself; for her own loss? Was she crying for Róisín, this woman who walked through life so lyrically? How could she have carried such a tattoo of grief across her heart, and then spend her life supporting other people to birth their babies?

'Eden was induced by medical staff before she was ready to be born. I told them repeatedly that she'd be born when she was ready. But you know, I was young and inexperienced. I didn't stand my ground firmly enough. Eden got stuck in the birth canal, and the shock of the obstetrician trying to pull her out was so traumatic that it ended up killing her. For years I didn't see it that way. I blamed myself.

36

The doctor was trying to save our lives, of course, but the problems began by interfering with the natural process and inducing me. It took me some time, and a *lot* of grieving and personal growth, to be aware that I could only heal my baby's birth by taking responsibility for it. I'd done plenty of blaming, but that's a different process altogether. This was about owning that I wasn't informed enough about birth, and about what a woman actually needs when she's in that mammalian place of letting a baby out of her body.'

Róisín pulled up outside her client's farmhouse. Topaz put her hand on Róisín's. 'I'm so sorry.'

'I know you are. I also knew you'd have an understanding because of your own experience. It's not something I tend to share with people. Grief is an inhospitable land for the general population. When I decided to give you the gift of coming to an antenatal session I had no idea of your background, but what I did know was how much my life has been transformed by pregnancy, birth and death, and that is what I wanted to share with you. Losing my baby taught me how to cry. That's a gift in itself, though most people wouldn't see the value of it.'

Glancing at her watch, Róisín said 'We've got a few more minutes till we need to go in. Topaz, just let your feelings come up.'

'I've never looked at life that way before, being a good British girl and all that!' Topaz laughed, trying to calm her nerves a little. *Why am I nervous?* she wondered.

'And remember: a pregnant woman's baby is listening to everything. Traditionally, it was the grandmother in a tribe or village who was asked by Spirit to be the midwife. It was, literally, her 'calling'. As time went on, the village midwife was also considered to be the psychologist, wise woman and herbalist of the place. The "go to" woman!' she laughed. 'The midwife isn't there to deliver a baby. Pizzas get delivered, not babes. They're born. I see myself as the guardian at the gate: protector of the sacred space. My job isn't to catch the baby and take all the glory, and I don't believe it should be the goal of any midwife to act in that capacity. That's just ego, and there's no place for that in a birth. Don't even get me started on the politics of birth. I say: keep the government out of the bedroom and leave women to birth without the advice of men in suits! My ethos in life is pretty simple: Have a home birth, and remove the need for doctors. Birth is as safe as life gets; it's an expression of sexuality. If anything needs to be healed, it is how women see their bodies.'

They both sat for a few minutes in silence. Topaz reflected on their conversation, absorbing it all, word by word.

Róisín opened the driver's door, and asked 'Coming?'

They walked up the white pebble path past the hollyhocks, blue delphiniums and stocks. A heavily pregnant woman greeted them at the door.

'Hi Róisín, come in!' She was bright and happy, and clearly looking forward to the visit. 'I've just popped the kettle on. Is this Topaz?' And she immediately reached out her hand. 'So lovely to meet you,' she smiled. 'I'm Camira.'

'Hello Camira, thank you so much for sharing this visit with me. I feel really honoured.'

Camira's kitchen was warm and inviting, and beautifully decorated. It benefitted from the extension of a large, wood-framed conservatory. An abundant bunch of Summer flowers stood in an old-fashioned, sky-blue porcelain pitcher on the wooden kitchen table. As the kettle whistled, Camira prepared a pot of tea.

'How have you been feeling?' Róisín asked, taking a freshly baked oat cookie from the plate before her, and catching crumbs.

'Fabulous. Those yoga classes have done wonders for my leg muscles,' she enthused. 'I'll be able to squat right through this birth.'

'Sleeping well? How are your dreams? Anything significant?' queried Róisín.

'I had a lovely one about a wild black stallion, actually,' Camira said excitedly. 'I was walking through a flower meadow, picking some to put in my basket; and he came galloping up to me. I wasn't scared. Somehow I knew he'd stop. He was friendly, and whinnied a bit as a greeting,' she laughed. 'And then, you'll never believe this,' she said dramatically, with expansive hand gestures. 'He kneeled down on one leg so I could get on, and then we rode away together. I don't know what it means, but it felt really beautiful.'

Topaz couldn't understand why Róisín would even ask about her dreams. What did that have to do with pregnancy and birth? *How odd*, she thought.

As if she was picking up her thoughts, Camira turned to her and said 'Róisín always asks me about my dreams. It's been a fascinating part of my pregnancy, well, since before pregnancy actually, and not something I expected when we started out, but it's really made a difference to understanding what's going on inside me.'

'Our dreams represent our subconscious,' Róisín

said, 'and are often an expression of our deepest thoughts and even of our unresolved issues. Analysing them can lead us to understanding ourselves better, and to facing up to our fears. This is vital in a conscious birth where a woman wants to take responsibility for how she brings her baby into this world.'

'The horse?' Camira asked. 'I've not had a horse dream before.'

'I would expect a horse dream about this stage in your pregnancy. He represents your wild nature; your sexuality. What's wonderful is that you weren't afraid of him in the dream. You met him head on. And then you and he symbolically became one by riding off together. As a midwife, it shows me that you're ready to give birth on every level.'

Topaz could see Camira grinning from ear to ear. 'You know, that's how I feel. There isn't a single part of me that's frightened of this birth. Jamie's built us a wonderful birthing pool. It's in the bedroom. Do you want to see?' she asked, but didn't wait for them to answer. Camira led them down the hall to an expansive bedroom with French doors leading to the back garden. A birthing pool was erected by the doors.

'What a beautiful place to give birth,' Topaz said; and realised how quickly her worldview on just about everything was changing. The garden was abundant with late Summer flowers. It struck her that Camira was going to be a great mother: she was clearly used to nurturing living things, as her garden was living proof. Looking around the bedroom, Topaz was touched by the simplicity and beauty of the space Camira had created: a place of calm and rest, a place to love and to be loved.

'Do you have the nursery ready?' Topaz asked.

Camira and Róisín looked at each other, and then burst out laughing. 'Our baby will sleep in bed with us; we're going to parent naturally. All mammals sleep with their babies at night.'

Topaz considered this for a few moments. 'I've never thought about it before, especially from the baby's point of view.' She paused again, 'Why would we separate a baby from its parents and leave it all alone in the dark?' she asked, answering her own question.

'Or put them behind bars!' added Róisín.

Camira walked over to her bedside table and picked up a book. 'You can borrow this, if you like. It's the only book you'll ever need to read on parenting again. Actually, the only book you need to read about what it means to be human!'

The Continuum Concept', read Topaz. 'Funny name for a book. What does it mean?'

'Long story,' Camira replied. 'Just read it.'

The three women returned to the spacious farmhouse kitchen and seated themselves around the table, sipping tea and nibbling at their cookies. Sunshine streamed in through the open stable-like door.

'Is there anything I can do to help you after the baby is born?' Topaz asked.

'We've got everything covered, but you know, if you're free, it might be lovely have a spare pair of hands after the birth so Jamie and I can just be together with our baby. My best friend will be away overseas, and Jamie's family lives way up north.'

'Of course. I'd love to,' she agreed; and was surprised by the excitement in her stomach.

'Camira, I'll just have a quick listen to babe's heartbeat while I'm here, 'Róisín added, pulling a pinard out her bag. Camira sat on the floral sofa in the conservatory part of her kitchen, and unbuttoned her blouse. Róisín placed the end of the pinard on Camira's pregnant belly for a while. 'Perfect. Everything's perfect.'

Topaz admired the pinard, a wooden trumpet-shaped instrument. 'I've not seen one of those before. They didn't use that when I was pregnant,' she added.

'Not many midwives do!' Róisín said. 'It's such a shame, as it makes for a far better midwife, and is safe for the baby.'

'I'll see you next week. Same time, same day okay for you Camira?' Róisín asked, looking into her diary.

'Yeah, great.'

Topaz leaned forward to hug Camira goodbye. 'Thank you so much for inviting me into your life in this way.' They smiled, both knowing deep down that this was the beginning of a lifelong friendship.

Camira hugged Róisín, and then waved them off at the door. Driving up the road, Topaz said 'I see why this isn't just a job! This is real heart-to-heart work: women's work.'

They were silent for a few minutes, and then she asked: 'Róisín, you had other children after your stillbirth? You mentioned a son.'

Beaming, she answered, 'Yes, a wonderful son. You'd like him, actually. He's just your type!' She smiled.

'What's my type?' Topaz asked curiously.

'Hmmm, it's just that you'd look good together,' she said mysteriously. 'I don't see him very often though. He lives abroad. He phones me every Sunday at lunchtime, though.'

'Wow, that's dedication.'

'No, that's love. He's very caring, and he's acutely aware of what a loss it was for me when he moved overseas so young. He did a degree, and planned on returning to Ireland straight after, but it never happened. He met someone...and well, that was the end of that.'

'Oh,' Topaz said, in a tone that showed she empathised.

Elm Tree Nursery

Topaz followed the wooden signs to Elm Tree Nursery. She'd heard of Francesca's nursery but had never been here before. An attractive piece of fertile land set on about four acres, it sidled up to the winding river. It was protected from the prevailing wind by elm, poplar and pine trees, and received sunshine throughout most of the day. Her car came to a halt on the pebble drive, by the front gate. A large piece of oak wood, engraved with the words *Elm Tree Nursery*, and a sketch of elm trees burnt into it, hung from a tree.

Topaz changed her sandals for sandshoes, and took in the scenery around her. Francesca had heard the car pull up and was jogging by the glasshouses to meet her. 'Hey, so glad you could make it,' she puffed lightly, beaming her bright smile. 'Shall we have a cup of tea before I show you around?'

'That'd be lovely,' Topaz agreed. Francesca led her to a small wooden hut, which served as an office. Filling the kettle, she turned to Topaz and said 'There's rain coming in later. You're timing is great. The Sun is spectacular this morning.'

After tea, they headed down to the polytunnels and glasshouses to look at the annuals and perennials, which were sold at farmers' markets, and then down to the fields, where there were herbs and wildflowers, and dozens of beehives. Many apiarists kept their hives here. *The best honey for 100 miles*, they said.

As they walked upon the rich black soil between the towering fennel and alliums, Topaz noticed that Francesca wasn't wearing any shoes. 'Doesn't it bother your feet walking on the dirt like that?'

'No. I'm used to it. I didn't enjoy it at first. It took

some getting used to. We spend our lives in shoes, with our feet blindfolded. There are so many nerves in our feet that it's a bit like cutting the whiskers off a cat. You know how they need whiskers to feel their way around? It's the same for humans. We need our feet to make sense of the world. For as long as humans have walked the Earth, they've been barefoot, they've sat on the ground, and they've slept on it. Many of man's ailments are because he's so disconnected from the Earth. I walk barefoot all the time when I'm here, and at home.'

Topaz laughed, and bent over to take off her shoes! 'When in Rome....'

'Every minute, lightning strikes the Earth about 5,000 times. That's a lot of voltage. Good electrons. And the more we tap into that, the healthier and more alive we feel,' Francesca said.

'Is that why you look so good? Is that why you have so much energy?' Topaz asked.

'I've never felt as good in my life as I do now... since I began the nursery. I loved the florist shop, but the difference between being indoors six days a week, under fluorescent lighting, next to electromagnetic radiation ~ you know: computers, mobiles, electrical gadgets and machines and so on, and this! This beautiful land, with soil, fresh air, sunshine? I wouldn't change it for *anything*. And you can't even get a Wi-Fi signal or mobile-phone coverage here. I love it! My paradise. Most people have no balance in their lives between technology and the natural world.' Francesca began cutting some flowers and created an impromptu bouquet, then passed it to Topaz. 'Here, for you.'

'Thank you so much. They're beautiful.' She slowly breathed in the scents.

'I've got some bulbs in the office, I'll get you some of those before you leave. Fancy a walk down to the river?' They headed off and spent some time chatting before Topaz had to leave.

'Best get back to work. Both of us!' she chuckled. They embraced, and went on with their day, pleased at the connection between them.

When she arrived home, Topaz divided the bouquet in two, and placed one of them on Sapphire's bedside table, and the other out in her studio. She looked at the illustration which she'd started yesterday, and saw it with new eyes. Lightning. *It needs lightning*, she smiled.

Daisies and Sunflowers

Francesca, aged 15

'Francesca! Get out! Get out of bed! The house is on fire! Wake up!' screamed her frantic mother, pulling the covers off the teenage girl's bed.

'Mum? What's going on?' she cried, half asleep, choking on the smoke-filled acrid fumes.

'We have to get out of here. The house is on fire,' she gasped, stifling a cough, 'Dad's outside with the baby. Hurry up!' Her mother pulled her through the smoky hallway, and they fought their way through the suffocating fumes until they reached the safety of outside air. Her father was crying, and the baby was screaming.

Sirens screeched down their street. All she could see was the red, red, red of five large fire engines with manic, staccato lights illuminating the street in the colour of devil red, and burly men dragging hoses across her front lawn. A confusing nightmare, surely. She'd wake up soon.

Neighbours peered out from behind their curtains. Others ran into the dark of night in their pyjamas, carrying buckets, impotently throwing water towards the fiery monster that had once been Francesca's safe place from the world.

Firefighters fought in vain to bring the ferocious flames under control, but it was too late. Nothing could be done. Francesca watched her whole life burn to the ground.

Local police found her family temporary accommodation.

Francesca was offered counselling to help her deal with the loss, but no-one could break through to her. The trauma indelibly etched itself into her growing bones. She shunned her friends, avoided the school dance, and cut out all her social groups. Not even her best friend could get through to her.

When work-experience week came around, the teachers tried hopelessly to find out what Francesca would like to do, but in the end decided to choose a workplace for her.

Mrs Daisy was a florist shop specialising in funeral flowers and tributes, and owned by an elderly lady. When Francesca turned up on day one, in her second-hand school uniform and scuffed shoes, Mrs Daisy sat her down in the kitchen at the back of the shop, and made her a cup of tea with toast.

'Rule number one,' she said kindly, her smile revealing dimples in her wrinkly cheeks, 'is never start the day without a full tummy.' It was quite obvious that the girl was wasting away. The teachers had warned the old woman that Francesca had closed down after the fire, and that this would be no easy placement. Mrs Daisy wasn't daunted. Her whole life was spent in the midst of people's grief, and she recognised that this was what Francesca was going through.

'You know, I don't think you should be in your school uniform while you're here. You're not at school. This week you're working as a florist's assistant so you should probably dress like one. I've got an idea. Come with me,' she smiled; and Francesca followed her out of the shop. Mrs Daisy put up a 'back soon' sign, and locked the front door behind her.

Together they walked up the main street of the small town and into a fashionable boutique. 'Hi Fern,'

Mrs Daisy said, greeting a young assistant. 'Could you help us find a few lovely dresses for my new helper, please? Nothing too frilly, these are work clothes and need to be practical. They can be pretty though,' she winked. Everyone in town knew that Francesca's family home had burnt to the ground, so when Fern was asked to help dress her, she scrambled around the shop picking out clothes that would not only fit her, but help her to feel like a new girl. Clothes befitting of someone making a fresh start.

Francesca's face remained expressionless as she tried on an assortment of dresses, blouses and skirts.

'We'll take all of them,' Mrs Daisy insisted, even though she knew there were way too many clothes for the purpose they came in for. She didn't mind. To her, Francesca was a broken flower, and if she had the stem clipped in just the right place, she could be put in water to continue blooming.

The elderly woman and her apprentice stopped for shoes on the way back to the florist shop.

Mrs Daisy showed the young girl the layout of the florist-shop floor, and where everything was stored. She introduced her to the flowers on display, and explained that the majority of bouquets she made were for people who were suffering emotionally.

Mrs Daisy showed Francesca how to change the water in the flower buckets, and to know when flowers were past their sell-by date.

She soon learnt where to find cards, ribbons, chocolates, teddy bears and an assortment of wrapping paper. In no time, she'd learnt how to operate the till and the credit-card machine.

The shrill ring of the phone shot through the air, and made both of them jump out of their skin.

'Yes, I see,' she said. 'They'll be ready for 3pm.

Would you like them delivered or will you collect them yourself?' When she hung up the phone, Mrs Daisy turned to Francesca. 'Can you help me with a job?'

The young girl, teetering on the edge of womanhood, nodded; her face still devoid of feeling.

'There's a young couple from the estate at the top of town who've lost their baby to a hospital infection, and we need to make a sympathy bouquet. Would you help me arrange one? Help me choose the colours and flowers? Can you do that?' she asked.

Francesca nodded. She'd been mute since the fire. Nothing anyone said made any difference. She walked around the small florist shop surveying the flowers, gently touching some; bending down to smell others. As she had already changed the water in all the buckets, she had a sense of where different flowers were, and which colours were in the shop, and which flowers smelled good and those which had no scent at all. *Imposters*, she named them silently. Instinctively, she selected six baby-pink lilies and a handful of asparagus fern. Mrs Daisy didn't interfere or advise; she just watched: A silent mentor to progress and purpose.

The mute girl turned to Mrs Daisy and asked 'May I use some ribbon and tissue paper with these, or would you prefer they were put into florist's foam?'

Mrs Daisy felt hot tears spring to her eyes. That young girl had asked her a question as if it was the most natural thing in the world; the same young girl who hadn't said a word to anyone in three, long months. She was a tender and vulnerable child on the verge of womanhood who had shut out the world, and locked herself in.

'The choice is yours my dear. This is your

bouquet. Every bunch of flowers that is made here isn't just a gift from the person who buys it, it's a gift from our heart. It says *we care*. So you arrange and decorate it just the way you like,' she said, and found it odd that she was so free with this girl. Inwardly she smiled, as she hadn't been so liberal with apprentices over the years, always going back and fixing the bouquets before the client arrived, to satisfy her perfectionistic tendencies. Today was different. These flowers were healing more than one person.

'It needs something else,' Francesca said, thoughtfully, her words as clear as scissors cutting through paper. 'Some lavender stems, I feel. It needs to smell relaxing.'

When she'd completed the bouquet to her satisfaction, Francesca wrapped the flowers carefully in a mix of pink and purple tissue paper, and tied them in silk fabric ribbon.

'This isn't going to stop that mama hurting, you know,' she said, with all the wisdom of an elderly woman. After a few moments of silence she added, 'But I guess it will help her to feel someone loves them,' she whispered.

'That's all we can ever do, my dear,' Mrs Daisy empathised, gently touching the top of Francesca's hand. 'Thank you for creating this. You've done a fine job.'

The phone rang again and again. It rang all afternoon with orders for the bereaved family. 'This is a busy day. We need to sit and have a nice cup of tea and a bite to eat before we continue. I'll put the kettle on,' she said, and headed up the few stairs to the kitchen at the back of the shop.

They ate in silence, with the radio on softly in the background featuring crooners from the 1950s.

Francesca tried to identify the smells in the shop, and made a list in her head: Coffee, freesias, roses, pine cleaning spray, eucalyptus leaves, paper, lavender, egg sandwiches.

'Can I make another bouquet?' Francesca asked, but didn't wait for an answer. She stepped from the kitchen into the front of the shop, flicking the skirt of her new floral dress like a little girl off to a party. Reading through the list of orders, she began at the top.

'I have a baby sister. She's one,' Francesca informed Mrs Daisy; and that's when the old woman realised the dam had been unplugged. Francesca talked all afternoon. At times she spoke so fast, the old woman wondered how she'd keep up with such loquaciousness. How do you stop a racehorse on the furlong? She told Mrs Daisy about her sister, her parents, her old bedroom, about the fire and the powerless firemen, about her school life, about her dreams to be a teacher, and anything else she could think of.

Mrs Daisy made a few bouquets herself, and then arranged them neatly into a large crate for delivery. 'Normally I'd just lock up shop while I deliver these. Would you like to come with me, or keep an eye on things?' she asked.

'I'll look after the shop,' Francesca said confidently. 'See you later.'

Francesca never returned to school after that work-experience week. Instead, she took on an apprenticeship with Mrs Daisy, though the old woman would be the first to say that Francesca was a natural with design, colour, and had an innate flair for recognising what needed to be said with any particular floral arrangement. She lost count of the times that Francesca taught her something new about flowers and people.

The childless old woman died five years later, and left *Mrs Daisy*, the florist shop and upstairs apartment, in her will, to Francesca. The legacy she left behind, though, was far greater than the bricks and mortar.

Francesca renamed the shop *Sunflower Express*, and painted the outside bright yellow, with a mural on one wall resembling Van Gogh's sunflowers. She never did forget the old lady who gave her the space to blossom.

Sketches

Topaz opened her emails.

FROM: *Ryland's Publishers*
Hey Topaz, got an interesting job for you if you're keen. We've got a new writer on our books. This is his first novel. It's for young teenagers, so we're after black-and-white line illustrations as well as the colour cover. I know you prefer to do full-colour illustrations for younger children's books, but I hope you'll give this some thought before saying "no" like you always do!!!!!!!!!

This writer has been involved with children's books for years. There probably isn't a book he hasn't read, and word has it that he's a big fan of your work. If he recommends a book it flies off the shelves. He runs a bookshop in the USA. The thing is, he's requested (ahem, <u>insisted</u>) that you do the artwork. He signed with us on the condition you did the artwork. Do me a favour Topaz? Say yes! My job's on the line. ~ Jacqueline.

Topaz laughed. She'd known Jacqueline since college and they often met up for coffee when she was down in London. She quickly replied.

REPLY, *Topaz Lane:*
What's his name, and why me?

FROM: *Ryland's Publishers*

He loves your work! He says you're "a unique voice in art who brings rare beauty to children's books…"

REPLY, *Topaz Lane:*

Hmmmm. I'll think about it. Send me the manuscript.

FROM: *Ryland's Publishers*

Pinging a PDF of the manuscript over to you right now! Get back to me by the end of business tomorrow. PLEASE. My boss is chomping at the bit. Love ya! J xxx

Topaz couldn't help smiling at her friend's mock drama. Jacqueline's father was her boss. There was no chance of her losing her job. Topaz downloaded the file and printed off the manuscript. When it was done, she made a cup of blackcurrant tea, and snuggled up on the cream-coloured corduroy sofa in her studio. Topaz never read any manuscripts online. She was an old-fashioned girl, and also vowed never to have a Kindle. *The work of the devil,* she once told an author who'd succumbed to the invention. She flipped straight to the back of the manuscript for the author's biography.

C. L. Murphy has owned The Children's Labyrinth, a popular New York specialist children's bookshop, for more than twenty years. This is his debut novel.

He lives in New York with two black cats, *Italics* and *Grammar.*

Thinking of her cat, Matisse, Topaz smiled, and wondered if all artist-types named their cats in relation to their work. *Something in common,* she thought.

Topaz returned to the front of the manuscript.

MOSAIC. *That's funny*, she thought, slowly taking in the name of the book, and then touching the small mosaic earrings hanging from her lobes. *How curious*, to have that for a title. She marvelled at the coincidence, and then began to read. Captivated from the first sentence, she didn't move until she'd finished the novel. She was struck by the similarities of Kate's 'digging deep' spiritual and emotional excavation terms and philosophy of life, and how this author was using the same descriptions. Did they know each other? Somehow, he masterfully wrote about such a heavy, to Topaz's mind, topic in a way that even she could understand! It all felt a bit too metaphysical, at first; but now this way of thinking was growing on her. Life was certainly more interesting, not to mention understandable, when she looked at the hidden meaning and multiple layers of life.

Topaz was sceptical about many things, but by the time she finished reading Mosaic, she knew that this was no coincidence. Meeting Kate like that; being encouraged not to hide her pain away; and then being asked to illustrate a book on this very theme? She suddenly wondered if there was such a thing as free will or if we were all just puppets in the game of life. How could she say no to this job? She raced to her computer.

REPLY, *Topaz Lane*:
Jacqueline, I'll do it! T xxx

A Nest Full of Eggs

Topaz, aged 15

Topaz sobbed as she walked home from school on the back lane by the old pine woods. The words her teachers had written in the report card kept playing over and over in her mind. 'Topaz daydreams too much. She'll never get anywhere in life unless she stops drawing. Too much time is spent doing sketches and not enough focus on mathematics and science. Maths: fail. Science: fail.'

'Why can't they see how well I can draw?' she said out loud to herself. 'And I passed English, music and humanities. Why don't they care about that?'

She sat down on the trunk of a fallen tree and reread the report card. Her parents would be so disappointed. 'How can my teachers say that I'll never get anywhere in life? They don't even know me!' She kicked at the pine needles on the ground.

After a while, she picked up her school bag and slowly wandered home, creating excuses to tell her parents. Lying abandoned in the grass, she spied a nest full of eggs, but no mother bird in sight. Bending down, she touched an egg to find it was stone cold. There would be no baby birds hatching from this womb-like basket of twigs. Topaz picked up the nest and carefully carried it home.

As she opened the front door, her mother called out, 'Hello darling, you're late home. There's some afternoon tea on the counter.'

'I'm not hungry,' Topaz muttered, and headed straight to her bedroom.

Mrs Lane let her daughter be for a couple of hours. She was normally such a happy girl, and clearly needed some space to deal with whatever was eating her up. Just before dinner, Mrs Lane knocked on Topaz's bedroom door. 'May I come in?'

'Sure,' came the solemn reply of a teenager with the weight of the world on her tender shoulders.

Mrs Lane sat on the bed, and looked at the artwork on the desk in front of Topaz. 'That's beautiful!' she exclaimed, and then noticed the bird's nest and eggs that she was using as her model, on the window sill.

'Are you sad because these eggs fell from the tree?' she asked kindly.

'No, I'm sad because my teachers don't value my art, and they think I'm not going to have a good life because I can't do maths and science,' she confessed, pulling her report card from her pocket. 'I'm sorry to disappoint you Mum,' she said, dropping her head in shame.

'My dear, we all have gifts in life. You've already found yours. That's a blessing, not a curse. You've got nothing to apologise for ~ not to me or to those teachers. I bet your art teacher couldn't sketch that nest of eggs as well as you have!'

The next morning Mrs Lane said to Topaz: 'Don't bother putting on your school uniform; we're going shopping.' They dropped Sapphire off at school, and headed off to the city. 'What are we doing, Mum?'

'You'll see,' Mrs Lane smiled. They walked through the arcade and into the town centre, and then stepped into Art Studio, a professional art-supply shop.

'Hello,' Mrs Lane said to the assistant. 'We'd like

to purchase everything a professional artist would need to set up their own studio. Pens, pencils, easels, brushes, charcoal, water colours, oils, paper of various textures, canvas....you name it, we want it.'

Topaz opened her mouth in shock. 'What are you doing, Mum?'

'No daughter of mine is going to fail at life because a bunch of teachers have no vision or instinct about an innate gift. Topaz, you could never disappoint me! I love you no matter what you do in life. I couldn't care less if you were a lawyer, a garbage collector, a nurse or a school caretaker. I simply want you to be happy. And if buying you a few pencils helps to put a smile back on your face, then that's what I'm going to do!' she said firmly, with a twinkle in her eye.

But of course, by the time they headed back to the car, they had more than a few pencils! Topaz didn't leave her room for weeks. Her mother applied to have her take an extended break from school on the grounds of 'mental health'. Every day that Topaz sat by her easel and created new art was another day that she blossomed more into who she truly was.

Three weeks later, Topaz burnt her report card. On the same day, her mother came back from the picture framer's shop with several of her pieces beautifully mounted, including *The Nest*.

Topaz spent another year in school, and then applied to a Fine Art School, where she stayed until her commissions were too many to make it practical to work full-time and study full-time.

Dinner under the Fairy Lights

Topaz was surprised how well she'd slept. She hadn't remembered sleeping so peacefully in a very long time. Often, at night, she'd lie awake for hours wondering 'what if?'. Glancing at the Sun coming over the nearby hills, she thought about tonight's dinner party. A giggle escaped her mouth in a way which pleased her. Fabulous new friends, and the possibility that they might just introduce her to a great new man. That, of course, made her very nervous! *But in a good way*, she chided herself.

Sapphire had been up for about an hour, and had already picked as many vegetables from the garden as her basket would carry. They both loved cooking, and often spent whole weekends in the kitchen making far more food than either of them could possibly eat. Not that any of the people on the dirt road to their house ever minded. Weekends, for them, often meant a casserole or cake landing on their doorstep.

Topaz showered, and then joined her sister in the kitchen. Tea was waiting, and they chatted for hours about *Mosaic*, and recent events in Topaz's life. She could feel Sapphire's shoulders almost melt with relief. Sapphire had been in a steady relationship for a number of years, but had never moved in with Jeff as she felt Topaz needed her. She never said this, but Topaz felt it in the air more than once. Sapphire was keen to start a family, but she knew the wound Topaz held needed to heal first in case it drove a wedge between them.

By mid-afternoon, all the food was prepared, and they were satisfied the evening would go well; food-wise, at least. Jeff was the first to arrive. He picked Topaz off the floor and spun her around like she was five years old. Topaz loved him like a brother, beard and all. He was an ecologically-aware architect, and they'd met when Topaz and Sapphire inherited the barn from their grandparents and needed it converted.

'There must be something I'm allowed to eat,' he pleaded when seeing all the food on the Aga and surrounding benches. 'Just a mouthful?'

'Just one!' Topaz laughed, offering him a small dish of cauliflower pilaf.

'A bit of that korma, too?'

'Cheeky!' She smacked his fingers, but Topaz didn't mind that he was so keen to try the food. His company was always fun, and he brightened up even the darkest days.

'Come and help us set the table in the garden!' she beckoned. The three of them carried out plates, cutlery, naan bread, cucumber raita, poppadoms, mango sauce, bowls of steaming rice, tandoori and chutneys. A small, oval-shaped muslin marquee was set up, with fairy lights, between the cherry trees.

Bluebell-scented beeswax candles, in hand-crafted terracotta pots, were staged up the centre of the long trestle table on an orange-coloured linen runner. They would comfortably be able to seat all the guests.

Róisín arrived first, and introduced them to Jez, her neighbour. He was a dapper young man, probably the same age as Topaz. She liked him immediately, but also sensed he was too much of a playboy for her liking. They laughed easily together, though, and she appreciated that. Róisín had brought a basket of home-made breads, and a posy of garden herbs: rosemary, thyme, lavender, sage and marjoram.

Lia and her husband's best friend, Lex, arrived at the same time as Annie and her father, George, and little Zac. Drinks of elderflower presse and white wine were passed around, and the conversation was light, friendly and fun. Francesca and Adam, her 'hot' seed supplier, ambled up the white pebble path. 'Great party! Sorry we're a bit late. Farmers and their cows blocking the road!'

Introductions were made, and Topaz noted that Adam was, indeed, hot. In fact, she couldn't take her eyes of him all night. It wasn't that she was actually attracted to him, as such, but that he was such a work of art. She really didn't see men like that every day! More than anything, she wanted to draw him.

Topaz passed them a tray with drinks, and invited everyone to take a place at the table. She popped inside to collect some of the hot meals, and turned the stereo on. Full-fat saxophone oozed out love songs into the early evening breeze.

'This is sooooo good,' was a phrase she heard over and over again that evening. 'You ladies should open a café!'

Topaz hadn't laughed so much for years. All of them were really lovely, genuine gentlemen, as her friends had promised. But even though she enjoyed their company very much, she knew in her heart that there would never be anything else, so when Adam asked her on a date later that night, she gently declined. He understood, and asked if she was interested in friendship. She'd never heard a man ask *that* before, and was delighted. A few days later they met for coffee, and she realised how lucky she was to have this man in her life, as a friend. She did, however, manage to get his clothes off…and draw him.

The Artist

Long before the Sun rose over the valley, Topaz was in her studio ready to work. She couldn't sleep. Again. This often happened when she was worried or anxious about her future: a future alone with no partner by her side, and no children; no nest full of eggs. Sleep also evaded her when she was excited about a project. *Mosaic* was just such a one. Topaz always refused black-and-white illustrations because she preferred colour. She still wasn't sure why she'd made an exception.

The morning passed quickly, and at 11am she stopped to make a cup of tea. It had been such a productive morning. At first, she was only going to do outlines for the publisher's approval, but many pieces completed themselves as if, they too, were in a hurry. She scanned half-a-dozen illustrations and emailed them to Jacqueline.

Instead of waiting for approval before continuing, she carried on anyway. She knew instinctively that these were right for the book. The storyline had gripped her straight away. Topaz had a knack for knowing which books would appeal to children. She was an old-fashioned girl at heart, and had greatly disliked the explosion of computer-generated graphics for children's books with block colours and no room for nuances in shade and tone. It was as if the innocence of childhood was no longer sacred, and that children were being hurried along on the conveyor belt of adult life.

Refusing to conform to latest trends in the children's book-publishing industry, and honouring her integrity, had actually put Topaz as publishers' choice. There were times that she was aware others might see her as some sort of prima donna, but for her, she knew that children's books were the love of her life, and she wasn't going to compromise.

From, *Ryland's Publishers*: Jack says the art is fabulous and to continue.

Topaz smiled. When had Jack ever not liked her work? The next week flew by, and she felt as if her project was nearing the end. A strange sense of disappointment fell over her. There'd be plenty more work, she knew that. Why did she want to keep collaborating with this author? Why had his words touched her so deeply, at such a primal level?

She felt a greater connection than with other authors. The words in the novel had seemed so powerful. It was as if the book had been written for her in some strange way. *Don't be stupid!* she said to herself, many times, when she reread certain chapters.

Looking at the clock, 4.30 on a Friday afternoon, she decided to spend the last half hour of her work day tidying the office: organising pencils, pens, paints, paper; putting away paperwork, bills, invoices; straightening her files; and watering the plants in the studio. She liked her workspace and home to be neat and in order.

Tavern Tunes and Saucy Salsa

Topaz stepped out of her salsa class on a high. She'd been going for four weeks, and had loved every second of it. Tonight she was meeting Lia so they could see Irish singer-songwriter, Mandy Bingham, in concert.

They met in Tarino's Tavern at 8pm, and ordered drinks. Topaz enthused about her dance classes, and said what a difference it had made to her Autumn to get out once a week even though the evenings were darker.

Gentle folk Americana ballads and acoustic guitar filled the room, and the audience fell quiet out of respect for the beautiful voice in their midst. Conversations could wait.

During the interval, they talked about music and how it fills the soul. Both agreed life would be utterly awful without the arts.

Afterwards, Topaz handed the singer a copy of her CD to sign. Feeling like a groupie, she smiled shyly and said 'Thanks so much. Love your work! Your voice and your lyrics hit me right here,' Topaz said, hand on her heart. 'So incredibly moving.'

Long after the music finished, Lia and Topaz sat in the bar discussing music, books, the weather, travel. Finally, Lia asked 'What do you want in your ideal partner?'

'You sprung that out of nowhere!' Topaz laughed. 'My ideal man is humorous, but serious when it matters. He's kind, thoughtful, gentle, but not emotionally weak. He has an artistic bent, and is passionate about his life. He doesn't eat animals, and he has strong views on the important things in life. He's ethical, charming and a lover of Nature.'

'You're describing yourself Topaz!' Lia laughed out loud.

'Am I?' she said, somewhat confused. 'Oh.'

'Shouldn't be too hard to find a man fitting that description,' Lia smiled.

'Did you know, when you met Carl, that he was "the one" for you?' Topaz asked.

'Yes, there was no question.'

'Oh,' Topaz said softly, then sipped her drink.

'Last drinks!' called the bartender.

'Shall we meet at Sam's bookshop on Tuesday for lunch?' Lia asked.

'Sure,' came Topaz's reply, but her thoughts were on the idea of love at first sight.

Market Day in the Village

'I'm just popping down to the shops, Saph. Do you want anything?' Topaz called out as she put the finishing lipstick touches to her lips. She assessed herself in front of the oval, oak-framed mirror in the kitchen.

'Olives!' her sister replied.

It was Saturday morning, and the town would be busy. Market day. Topaz generally spent her work week alone, which was how she liked it, but on Saturdays she traded solitude for buzz, and treated herself to breakfast in her favourite café, which was also a small bookshop. She was friends with the owner, Samantha. Saturday mornings were too busy for Sam to stop and chat for long, but they always had time for a hug and to have a quick catch-up. Sam's Bookshop was built in 1709 in the Stuart era, the time between James the first and Queen Anne. There were low wooden beams, and open fireplaces. At any time of the year, it was a cosy haven from the bustle of town.

Topaz decided that as it was such a gloriously sunny Autumn day, she'd have her coffee outside at one of the wrought-iron tables overlooking the churchyard headstones and gardens. The mature English trees, now losing their rust and mustard-coloured leaves to the breeze, offered a peaceful space in the middle of town. Church bells chimed, encouraging little girls in tutus to hurry to their ballet class. Other children scampered to the library, like dogs on leads, dragging parents in their wake. Topaz pulled out her notebook and started scribbling down ideas for the cover of Mosaic. Her brain had been buzzing with them since reading the manuscript. It had been a new venture for her: black-and-white illustrations after years and years in watercolour. The sketches were almost complete, and now she could focus on her first love: colour covers.

Topaz had a sudden burst of inspiration, and the joy of it caused her to look up from her notepad. A tall man, casually dressed in faded-blue jeans, purple, long-sleeved t-shirt and chunky, olive-green cable-knit cardigan, was walking along the sandstone pavement in her direction, and it was like she'd known him forever; but she didn't know his name. *Who is he?* She asked herself. *Where do I know him from?*

He couldn't unlock his eyes from hers, either, and gave her a broad smile. She felt the colour rise in her cheeks, as if she were a schoolgirl with a crush on her gym teacher and had just been found out. And then she jumped right out of her skin when a familiar voice said 'Hi Topaz! How nice to see you!' It was Róisín, bright as ever. She bent down and kissed Topaz on the cheek. 'I'm so glad we bumped into you. This is my son, Connor. He's made a surprise visit.'

Topaz was sure words wouldn't come out of her mouth; but he spoke first. That accent, oh that accent! Irish, like his mother. 'So very pleased to meet you, Topaz. My mother hasn't stopped talking about you since I arrived.' He tilted his head down in acknowledgement.

'All good, I hope?' she asked nervously, conscious of her pink cheeks betraying her feelings.

'Oh yes.' His smile had her melting into the pavement. Couldn't she just start her life here? Walk into the sunset together? Have half a dozen children with those cute Irish accents. She wondered if Róisín could see the heat in her cheeks. *Was it obvious to him, too?*

'I'm afraid we must dash; I need to get a couple of things. I'll call you as soon as I hear from Camira. She'd love you to come and meet her husband before the birth. Is that okay?'

'Yes, absolutely. Wonderful.' But her eyes weren't on Róisín. They were on Connor.

'Very nice to meet you, Topaz. I hope we'll see each other again,' he said, as if the fact that he didn't live locally meant nothing.

'And you, too. Goodbye,' she smiled, shyly. Finally, she could breathe again.

Topaz sat back down to her now cold coffee, and then had the urge to look up and see where they were walking to. Their eyes locked on each other. He had turned around too. They both laughed out loud. *Caught!*

Her hands were shaking like the Autumn leaves falling in the air. Why was she nervous, for goodness sake? This was silly! How could a complete stranger have her turning to jelly? Topaz headed home. She had to tell someone!

Sapphire was laughing hard as they sat at the kitchen table. 'See, there *is* life in the old girl yet!'

'But he lives overseas. It's not like I'll ever get to see him again.'

'I'm sure Róisín would give you his number. You could skype each other!'

'Skype makes everyone look like alien goats. I'm not skyping! And besides, I can hardly skype a stranger and say, by the way, you made me go weak at the knees!'

'Why not?' Sapphire asked, as if skyping was the most natural thing in the world.

'I'm not having a conversation with someone via a computer camera,' Topaz insisted. 'Jeff coming over later?' she asked, changing the subject.

'Yeah. Thought we'd watch a movie tonight. Want to join us?'

'Thanks, but I want to finish a commission, so I'll head to the studio and work on that,' Topaz said.

She turned thoughtfully to her sister. 'It's time you and Jeff moved in together. I know you both want to. You can't shield me forever from the big, bad world. I've got to stand on my own two feet. He'd marry you in a heartbeat, Sis. Say yes.'

'Topaz! Where's all this coming from?'

'Jeff's a great guy. *You're* great! I'm in the way. Please. Tell him he can move in here or you in with him. Whatever choice you make is fine. I'll go with the flow.'

Jeff had already built his home, with Sapphire and their future children in mind. He'd even built a den and a tree house in the garden four years ago. All they needed was to have the children.

Sapphire sensed a huge change in Topaz. She couldn't pinpoint what it was. Salsa classes? Surely not the man she'd just met on the street! No, it was more than that. It had been blossoming in recent weeks. Maybe it was since her birthday lunch? Yes, that was it.

'I'll think about it,' Sapphire promised, feeling excitement almost bursting out of her chest.

An Ordinary Day

'Hi Topaz, I'm wondering if you'd like to arrange a day to receive your birthday gift? I know it's a bit late, but we've both been rather busy. Would tomorrow work for you to come over? Annie asked.

'Sure,' Topaz replied. Cradling the phone against the crook of her shoulder, she poured a cup of tea. 'What time?'

'Why don't you come for breakfast and spend the day with Zac and I?'

'Great, I look forward to it.'

Topaz arrived to the smell of pancakes with blueberries. 'I picked these berries from the garden this morning,' Zac announced proudly.

'These are the best pancakes I've ever eaten, Zac,' declared Topaz, savouring every mouthful. 'Did you help your mum make them?'

'Yes!' he beamed brightly.

Annie introduced Topaz to their gentle homeschooling life. They ate a leisurely breakfast, then went outside to stack firewood for an hour or so. When they came inside for a hot drink, Zac made himself comfy on the sofa by the woodstove and read for a while.

'In the mornings, Zac reads and does some workbooks while I make this silver jewellery,' Annie said, opening a large box to reveal exquisite rings, earrings and brooches. 'I sell online, but we travel to markets to sell them at stalls, too.'

'I didn't realise you had a job,' Topaz said, intrigued by the jewellery before her.

'Being a single mum, I need to balance earning

an income with being a parent. This works well for both of us.'

'Do you follow the national curriculum or have tutors for him?' Topaz asked, wondering how a mother would recreate school lessons in the home.

' We take a very free-range approach to learning. Zac is the best teacher as he knows what he needs, and what he wants to learn. I'm here if he needs support. We aim for a relaxed life.'

'Sounds heavenly,' said Topaz, smiling and reflecting on her own not-so-idyllic school days.

'It's not a perfect lifestyle, but it suits us. Here, try this on,' Annie said, passing Topaz a beautiful silver beaded bangle. 'Hey, that really suits you. You're welcome to keep it if you like.'

'It's gorgeous. Thank you so much,' she said, moved by the kind gift. They sat at the table for a couple of hours, and Annie threaded together silver and glass beads for bracelets and necklaces. They talked about their childhood, their parents, their dreams, their hurts and their hopes.

Zac was content, in a world of his own, building towers from wooden blocks; and drawing. Sometimes he wandered outside, collecting sticks and twigs for the town he was building on the lounge-room floor.

'Ready for lunch?' Annie called to Zac. She cleared the jewellery off the table and transformed her industrious workspace into a beautiful eating area, with a vase of fresh flowers, cotton tablecloth and a candle.

Zac collected spoons and bowls for the table, and Annie brought over a pot of soup she'd prepared first thing that morning. Zac and Annie said a small prayer of gratitude, and they all began to eat.

72

After lunch, Topaz washed the dishes, and then they all headed off for a walk by the river. Topaz and Zac had pebble-skimming competitions and raced each other up the path towards the woods. The Autumn chill didn't deter them. Sunlight, fresh air, and a couple of hours in Nature invigorated all of them. When they returned home, Annie relit the fire and sat down to read some of *The Secret Garden* to Zac. Topaz smiled at the beautiful way that Annie lifted the words off the page so that she was truly being a storyteller. Topaz admired the beautiful bond mother and son had created.

At the end of four chapters, Zac declared that he was off to play with his train set. Annie and Topaz prepared some steamed vegetables and rice for dinner, and Annie's dad, George, came by to say hello. That evening, when Zac was tucked up in bed, Topaz said to Annie, 'You know, many single mums don't have it easy, but you make it look like a piece of cake. How do you do it?'

'Well, it's not a piece of cake. I'm always having to budget, and to balance my needs with Zac's needs.'

'How do you do that?' Topaz asked, curiously.

'I'm blessed to have my dad living over the road, but I don't use him to babysit or to rescue me. He's there for moral support and to play trains!'

'That sounds like a good use for a grandfather!' she said.

'What I've learnt is that I need to parent from the heart; to parent in a way that feels right for me and Zac, and not the way all my friends think I should.'

'That must be hard to go against the grain,' Topaz wondered, aloud.

'When you follow your heart, it's not that hard. I like our simple lifestyle. We don't have much money or a fancy house or car, but what we do have is filled with love.' Tears welled up in her eyes. 'That's worth more than anything. Being a mum has made me a stronger person. I feel like a lion most of the time, ready to roar and stand my ground if someone steps in to criticise. It's not a sin being a single mother or a young mother. I have just as much love in my heart as a rich, middle-class, middle-aged married woman. You know, Topaz, you've never asked me why Radio Birch picked me as one of the women for your *Does-Life-Begin-at-Forty?* lunch date.'

'That's true. How *did* you get chosen?' she asked, shocked that it hadn't even occurred to her how the station had rustled up five amazing women.

'I went to school with one of the researchers on Josh Landing's show. A few weeks before the competition, she came round for lunch. We were talking about her work and how she was under pressure to find five women to be part of this competition, and she said *'Your life's interesting, and you're nowhere near forty, would you go to lunch?'* And I said, *'Free food? Yes please!'* But of course, I had no idea how amazing that lunch would be ~ and not just the food ~ or how incredible it would be to meet such diverse women. I didn't know the other women, apart from Róisín, who I'd recommended to Radio Birch, but I did recognise a couple of them, as I've lived here most of my life.'

'It's such a small world, isn't it?' Topaz marvelled. 'You just never know who you'll meet, and how they'll change your life.'

Cartoons

Zac and Topaz had already met a few times before, and really enjoyed each other's company, but when she came over on Friday evening this was one of the few times he'd been left with a childminder before, apart from his grandfather. Annie knew that Topaz and Zac were good for each other, and was more thrilled about their evening together than going on a date. 'There's plenty of food in the fridge, and this is Dad's number if you need anything urgently. Thanks so much, Topaz. Have fun Zac. Give Mum a hug!' They hugged tightly, and Zac went to get his new puppy to show Topaz. 'This is Max. He's eight weeks old. Do you like dogs?' he asked.

'Well, I'm more of a cat person, actually. I guess it's what you get used to, isn't it? But he sure is cute! Where did you get Max?' she asked, roughing up his fur.

'He was the runt in the farmer's litter. Mum says runts need the most love.'

'Your mum is right,' she said, patting the excited puppy. 'Hey, shall we draw Max?'

Topaz pulled a sketch pad from her backpack. She drew several pictures of the dog, some lifelike and others in cartoon style. Zac was delighted. 'Can I keep them?' he asked.

'Sure you can. Here's some paper. Would you like pencil or pen?' she asked.

Zac used pencil, and was rather nervous, but he soon got used to drawing, and Topaz wasn't at all judgemental like he thought a famous artist would be. 'My friends go to school, and they're always telling me that the teachers say they should draw like them.

And they tell them what colours they can use. And then my friends say that to me when I'm drawing… Mum never tells me how to draw,' he said.

'Well, I love your drawings Zac. And I bet Max does too!'

They spent the evening chatting easily, like old friends. Topaz's heart warmed at his innocence and the free way he opened up to her. She wondered how children go from that state to the one in adulthood where they're emotionally closed down and suspicious of everyone.

It wasn't long before Topaz was tucking the young boy in bed. She bent over and kissed him on the forehead, and she felt a welling up in her chest. How easy it was to love a child, even if he wasn't your own. 'Sleep well, Zac.'

'That's what my mum says,' he smiled. 'And she says *I love you*,' he hinted.

'I love you, Zac,' Topaz said, and was stunned by how good she felt inside. *Is this what being a mother is like*, she wondered, *having your heart blown wide open?*

'I'm so glad we're friends, Zac. Goodnight.'

'Will you come back and draw with me another night?' he asked, as if her answer would reveal the truth about how she felt.

'It's a promise,' she smiled, and turned the light out.

It was another few hours before Annie returned home, flushed with the thrill of her first post-birth date. 'I'll tell you about it next time we meet,' she promised. 'Go home and get some sleep. It's late. Thank you so much,' she said.

'No, Annie. Thank *you*. I had the best time.' Topaz grabbed her bag, and quietly headed out the front door. 'Bye.'

On the Widow's Doorstep

Annie, aged three weeks

The young, pale woman hunched over the Moses basket, and leaned in to kiss the sleeping infant bundled up against the chilly weather. 'Stay safe,' she whispered. Her body remained numb as she rang the doorbell. There, on the steps of a widow's front door, she left her baby. The young mother walked away and deliberately didn't look back.

Postnatal depression had mercilessly pulled her into a deep, dark and dangerous abyss. Her husband worked long hours to pay the bills, and came home weary, late at night. The birth had been traumatic, with the baby cut out of her womb and then placed in a hospital nursery surrounded by a dozen screaming infants. The young mother begged to be reunited with her baby, but the hospital staff insisted she get some sleep, and leave the baby to them. They said they'd feed her from a bottle. They told her not to bother with breastfeeding until she was feeling brighter. But she never did.

After three weeks, in the dead of Winter, she could take no more of the isolation; of the baby's incessant cries; of standing in the icy little kitchen, heating formula in the night; and of the loneliness. She was always lonely. In her heart she felt that the baby deserved a better chance at life.

She walked away, without looking back; and she never returned.

The grieving widow, deep in mourning, was in no state to bond with a stranger's baby. Empty-hearted, she took the hungry infant to the local orphanage. Despite a frantic search by police, another week was to pass before the baby was reunited with her father.

Leaving the city of his birth, the young, vulnerable father took his baby with him to the country. Wages would be lower, he knew that, but so would the cost of living. He hired a live-in nanny to be with the baby, and to provide a constant caretaker whom the little girl could grow to love. Life as a single father was hard. Excruciatingly hard. But during the years that followed, father and daughter developed a great bond of love and appreciation for each other. Annie never quite became reconciled with the idea that a mother could just abandon her baby. That she could just walk away; just like that, without so much as a word of 'help'. To this day, she didn't know if her mother was dead or alive.

When Annie found herself pregnant to her first boyfriend, at 16, it felt as if the world came crushing down around her. He insisted she have an abortion, but Annie refused. If there was anything she knew about herself, it was this: she was not going to be like her mother! But she found that old wound of abandonment resurfacing in the form of her boyfriend, who disappeared from her life without a trace; pulling open the deep scab of Annie's long-term wound.

Annie's father stepped in and supported her throughout pregnancy and parenting. He found a lovely Irish midwife by the name of Róisín, who lived nearby, and hired her to come and attend Annie at home. It was a healing time for father and daughter, and little Zac brought much love and laughter into their lives.

Writer's Block

Topaz and Lia had met up at Sam's Bookshop and Café a couple of times in the past week. Welcoming and warm, it was a cosy place to meet for a quick lunch. Being self-employed, and experts at self-discipline, they knew they could afford the luxury of lunches out without it affecting their output too much. They had so much to talk about, and their shared love of the publishing world meant no shortage of conversation. They often sat in the bookshop going through their favourite titles and the stories behind the authors.

'Have you started writing in your journal yet?' Lia asked curiously. 'Started creating a new life?' she smiled.

'Actually, I have. Nothing major... no novels or deep insights,' she said. 'Mostly I'm just writing down things that I'm grateful for, just like you suggested,' Topaz confided.

'That's why you look so different! I knew it,' Lia said excitedly. 'You've seemed like such a different person from the day we met.'

'Like someone let the genie out of the bottle?' Topaz asked curiously. 'Yes, something has changed. I can't pinpoint what it is, though. I'm also working on a project that's really had me thinking about my life: about pain, loss, and moving onwards. It's a book for kids, but it's so profound. Lia, I've never read anything like it before. I feel like it was written for me. The distilled message is that you can't heal what you can't feel. It encourages children to share their emotions. Can't see many parents or teachers liking that too much!'

They both laughed at the thought of it. 'But it's

really given me food for thought, particularly about the way I bottle up emotions.'

Lia shared that a fellow writer was complaining about writer's block, but Lia thought there was no such thing. 'People think it's a lonely life, being a writer, but I find life is lonely if I don't write,' she said, sipping her latte. 'We all have many lives within this life. They come in episodes: birth, infancy, childhood, first job, university, mothering, career, mid-life crisis, menopause, retirement, old age and death; but you know, life isn't about our chapter headings! Most people think life is a series of exclamation marks which punctuate weddings, divorce, babies, teenagers, mortgages, foreign holidays, promotions and so on. I reckon the real highlights of life are to be found in each single sentence on the page. But then I would say that, wouldn't I? I'm a writer!' she laughed.

'Do you prefer your move into fiction after starting off in journalism?' Topaz asked.

'I enjoy both, but for different reasons. Stories are medicine, a kind of homeopathy of the heart, and we can learn just as much from a work of fiction as from any highbrow thesis,' Lia added. 'Time for another coffee?'

A Sister Slipped Away

Lia, at nineteen

At 19, Natalia changed her name to Lia. She knew it was time to carve a new identity: One that didn't involve being 'just' the big sister of a teenager who'd had enough of life. It was Lia who found the limp and lifeless body hanging from an old rope in her father's wooden toolshed.

It was Lia whose blood-curdling screams dragged the neighbours from their television sets. And it was Lia who spoke so eloquently about her beautiful sister at the funeral. Her tribute, which she'd written in the dark of the night, left the congregation in tears. She'd opened everyone's heart with her wisdom, but felt herself rapidly closing down.

Lia had just begun dating, and was about to start on a journalism degree. The family tragedy wasn't much fun for her hormonally driven boyfriend, who had hoped for a good-time girl, not a misery guts. Maybe it was his age, maybe it was his temperament, but Matt just didn't understand the impact this had on Lia or her family. When were they *ever* going to get back to normal?

After a few months, she dropped out of her journalism course and packed her backpack. Despite the tearful farewell, she set off on a trip around the world, telling her family she'd be back in six months. She just needed time and space to get her head together. Six months turned into ten years, and when Lia returned she was a different person to the young girl they'd kissed goodbye. In her absence she'd travelled all around the world, and had written about her experiences. Selling articles to newspapers and magazines, Lia carved herself a name as a writer, not just on travel themes, but on the human experience.

After five years, she met the man who would be her husband and the father of her three children. In time, they returned to Cumbria, and she settled down in the valley. Using her time as a stay-at-home mother to forge a career as a novelist, writing was Lia's best friend: A companion who would listen to her no matter how she was feeling or how much pain wrenched her heart muscles. Writing was her mentor, her shrink, her confidante. Her book, *My Stolen Sister*, became an instant, international best seller. Only Lia's close friends and family knew it was autobiographical and not a work of fiction.

Ryland's Publishers

The phone ringing nearly made Topaz jump out of her skin. 9am. *Wow, someone's starting work on time*, she thought, rescuing the phone from its cradle. 'Good morning, Topaz Lane.'

She recognised the voice at the end of the line immediately. It was Jacqueline.

'What are you doing today?' she asked frantically down the line.

'Er, good morning to you too! What's wrong?'

Jacqueline was tripping over her words. 'The author wants to meet you. Today,' she said.

'Which author?'

'Mosaic. C. L. Murphy! My boss wants you here today to meet up, no matter what it takes. Can I order your train ticket now? I just have to press 'pay' and you're ready to go, right?' she asked, her computer mouse hovering on the Rail Easy website.

'I don't even meet most authors, unless there's a book launch. What's the fuss with this one?'

'The author is only here for the rest of the day… anyway, can you get the 10am train?'

'Blimey girl, you're lucky I'm already at work! Yes, I'll be there. Will you have time for a coffee afterwards?'

'Sure!' and they hung up at the same time.

Authors, she muttered, *and they think artists are the temperamental ones!*

Topaz hurriedly changed into a suit, then drove to the station.

The train pulled into Euston at 1pm. Topaz had brought some of the illustration samples with her, but she'd already sent them all by email, so was at a loss to understand why she had to be there in person. The author had asked for her specifically. Surely she wasn't going to be fired from the project!

Jacqueline met her in the lobby. 'Jack's in his office with the author now. Go on in.' They gave each other a quick hug. 'See you later?' Topaz asked, feeling incredibly nervous about what lay before her.

Knock, knock.

'Come in!' Jack's warm voice echoed back.

Topaz took in a deep breath. *Calm yourself, girl. Calm!* She entered hesitantly.

And there, standing side by side with Jack, were those Irish eyes. Topaz Lane didn't know which way to look, but her heart made her keep looking into his eyes.

'Connor? *You're* C. L. Murphy? Why didn't you say anything when we met?' She found herself wanting to be cross but not quite able to. Had he deliberately been deceptive?

'I'll just go and get us some coffees,' Jack interrupted with a smile on the corner of his lips, as he sensed the chemistry. 'Have you had lunch, Topaz?'

'No,' she replied, keeping her eyes firmly on Connor.

'I'll rustle some up.' And with that, he disappeared out of the office.

'I'm sorry. It just didn't seem right to mention it when I was with my mother. She doesn't know I've written a book, and I'd rather she didn't know until it was actually published. Can you keep a secret?' he smiled.

'How do you expect me to spend time with Róisín and not say anything?' she demanded, feeling hot under the collar. 'Do you mean you came over for a business meeting and she thinks you came home to see her?'

'Women aren't the only ones who can multi-task.' Connor was smiling, and she knew, just *knew*, what he was thinking.

'Don't you dare! Don't you dare say I look beautiful when I'm angry!'

'How did you know what I was thinking?' he teased.

Her only retort was: 'Your mother loves you so much. You've no idea how much she misses you. And you, business trip! Men!'

His smile was dimming.

'I'm sorry you feel that way.'

'And why me? Why the desperation to have me illustrate your work? There are plenty of artists who could do a fine job.'

'Yes, there are. But they're not you,' he answered.

'What's that supposed to mean?' she asked, wondering why he was still smiling when she was becoming increasingly furious.

'Anyone worth their salt knows you're the best in the business. I wanted the best. It's pretty simple.'

'No-one but no-one gets to "demand" their artists. What makes you so special?'

'Topaz, if you want something in life, you just have to ask for it,' he said with all the charm of a purring cat. 'If you *really* want it, that is...' He sat down in the chair. 'I've seen the illustrations that you sent through. They're wonderful. Just as I'd imagined in my head when I was writing the story. I knew you'd be able to do that: That you'd read my mind.'

And there was that smile again. That same smile that had her shaking like a leaf and weak-kneed outside Samantha's Bookshop and Café.

85

'It's my job to see what the author's writing, Connor. And why am I here? Why did you have to meet me so urgently?'

'Because I wanted to *see* you again.' His smile made her heart flutter far too quickly for comfort. 'I'm flying out tonight, and I hoped you might join me for dinner first. If that's not too presumptuous of me?' he said. His lyrical and whimsical Irish accent played upon the rolling 'r', and rolled straight into her heart.

'And what about your wife? Won't *she* mind you having dinner with me?' Topaz retorted.

'My wife?' he asked, raising his eyebrows.

'Here we go, some ploughman's on rye, and fresh coffees,' said Jack, placing them on his desk. 'They're from the café downstairs. They're pretty reliable. Hope you like them.'

'Right, where were we?' he asked. Jack Ryland was in his sixties, grey around the edges, and had been in the publishing business since he was fifteen years old. Ryland's started as a small family publisher, but now had a worldwide reputation for quality children's literature.

'So, Topaz, Connor is absolutely delighted with your artwork. So are we! I see you've finished the internal drawings. Do you have a rough time-frame of when you might have finished the cover? We're hoping to launch the book for mid December, in time for Christmas. It's all edited, proof read, and layed out; it just needs to have the pictures inserted.'

'I can be finished this week, Jack,' she said firmly; but Topaz was feeling infuriated. *First Connor lies to his mother, then he wants dinner with me behind his wife's back.* She wanted to stamp her feet in protest.

'Is there anything else, Jack, or can I go now?' she asked, as if he'd put her on detention.

'Go? I thought the four of us could have dinner tonight before Connor flies home,' Jack said, almost pleading. 'Please. Jess has made up the bed in the spare room, so you don't have to catch a late train back.'

She could feel Connor's eyes looking at her, waiting for her to give the green light.

'Please?' he added, a smile at the corner of his lips.

'Fine. But first I need to catch up with Jacqueline.'

'Meet us in the lobby at seven, and we'll go together,' said Jack, feeling rather pleased with himself. Topaz turned on her heels, barely muttering good-bye.

'Don't you want your sandwiches?' Jack called out to her disappearing silhouette.

She caught Jacqueline's arm in the hallway. 'Why was I called here?' she demanded.

'Connor wanted to meet you!' she said, feeling defensive.

'He *has* met me! At home! I know his mother. I'll be back at five and we can meet for coffee,' she said. She stomped down the hallway and out onto the busy street.

Topaz caught her reflection in a shop window. She could see the steam coming out of her ears, still furious with Connor for lying to her.

Was he stalking her? She wondered. But she knew in her heart that this wasn't true.

If there was anything Topaz wasn't going to do it was have a fling with a married man. She knew what it was like to be on the receiving end of infidelity, and it didn't matter how gorgeous and devastatingly handsome Connor Murphy was, he was not going to be the exception to her firmly-in-place rule. No, no, *no!* No amount of that lyrical Irish brogue would make her budge. And then, as she looked at how her auburn hair was held tightly up in a bun, and at the freckles on parade across the top of her nose, somehow the purple business suit didn't seem right for dinner. She hadn't been expecting to stay in London for the evening, and now she was going out to dinner. She could wear the suit, but a nagging voice inside her dared her to live a little and spend some of her hard-earned money on a beautiful dress. *A dress? What for?* she chided herself, as she walked into a small boutique. The owner rushed to her side, eager to dress such a delightful-looking woman.

'I just want something simple. No lace. No frill. No girly-girly,' she said, realising she sounded more like a drill sergeant. 'I'm sorry. Long day. I just want…' and was starting to sigh when the woman said 'I have just the thing. Come with me.'

She pulled out a dress in the colour of holly-berry red.

'It's red!' Topaz spat, horrified. 'I'll look like a...'

'Try it on before you make that judgement. You can't tell anything about a dress when it's on a hanger.'

Topaz took the dress and reluctantly tried it on in the spacious changing rooms. The lights were designed to sell dresses. No life-stripping fluorescent in here…but subtle illumination and kind mirrors.

Topaz looked at the line of the dress. It came to her mid-calf, and hung, handkerchief-style, around her long legs. Cinched in at the waist, and cupping her breasts, it was plunging v-shaped with short sleeves.

'Try this on with it,' came the assistant's voice from the behind the curtain. She handed her a silver pendant.

'Wow, that really does look good on you!' she said, sounding impressed. 'I knew it would, but it looks even better than I thought. Turn around,' she suggested.

Topaz reluctantly turned around, and had to admit that she didn't look tarty, but like a real woman. A curvaceous woman. She took a deep breath. Dresses like this had no place in her life. She always dressed for work, even though she knew she could turn up to her own studio in pyjamas. Dresses like this were simply not needed. *And I don't need one now*, she thought.

'Most women have a little black dress, but very few can wear a little red dress and look like this. I'm not saying this because it's my job. I'm saying it because you'll feel different when you go out in it. Take my word on this. The clothes we wear represent a part of our personality, and sometimes there are parts of us that we don't let out very often. I get the feeling that you don't let the sensuous and sexual woman see the light of day too many times in the year. Please don't take that the wrong way. It's not an insult. I promise! Buy this dress, and if you don't come away from your date feeling one-hundred per-cent stunning, I'll give you a refund. I'll put it in writing.'

Topaz couldn't understand why the woman was bending over backwards. 'Who says I'm going on a date?'

The assistant raised her eyebrows. 'There's a great hairdresser two blocks from here: *Shivani's*. Ask for Leonie. Tell her I sent you. She'll do your hair. Show her the dress. Leonie will know what to do.'

Topaz found herself pulling out her purse. 'I hope I'm not going to regret this.'

'You won't,' the assistant winked.

Topaz had coffee with Jacqueline, who listened intently to Topaz's complex mixture of emotions.

'You could pull out of the contract,' she mused.

Topaz was horrified. 'Why would I do that?' she asked.

'I'm just saying…if he's so darned awful, why collaborate?'

'Did I say he was awful?' she asked, wondering how to backtrack.

'Your hair, by the way, looks amazing!' Jacqueline smiled. 'Anyone would think you were going on a hot date! Not wearing your business suit, are you?'

'As a matter of fact, I'm not.' She carefully opened the pink cardboard box where the red dress had been neatly folded.'

'Oh my! You *are* going on a date!'

'He's married. Don't be silly. You know I'd never go there…'

'Who said he's married?'

'His mother.'

'Hmmm, I didn't know that,' she said, looking a bit confused.

Lady in Red

The two couples, dressed to the nines, met in the lobby of Ryland's, right on 7pm. Topaz greeted Jess first with a kiss on the cheek. They were more like friends than the fact Jack was her publisher.

'Shall we go?' Jack asked. 'You look divine, Topaz. Just divine! You sure scrub up well when you put your mind to it.' He gave her a hug. 'Are you in a better mood than you were this afternoon?' he chuckled.

'What's so funny?' she demanded to know.

'Jack's right,' Connor said, diffusing the tension. 'You look divine. May I?' he asked, taking her hand and gently kissing her skin. 'I think we're the luckiest men in town, Jack, having an evening with these lovely women!'

'There's the cab I ordered,' said Jack. It was large, and they all sat in the back. Topaz was sitting side by side with Connor. She could feel their thighs touching. *He's married. Stop it!* Her mind was racing, but not nearly as much as her heart.

The four of them made small talk, and were soon at the restaurant. It was an intimate place, with private alcoves, but not so private that half the guests didn't stop Jack to say hello! He was well-known around the city.

The evening was far more pleasant than Topaz expected. She'd greatly enjoyed catching up with Jess, who had been a silent mentor through her early years with Ryland's, offering her the female touch alongside the male-dominated world of contracts and deadlines.

'So, Topaz, our US partners are going to launch Connor's book in his shop. Jess and I are going to the launch, and I wondered if you'd like to join us? After all, you're integral to the book, too. As you know, Jess and I have an apartment we keep in New York for my business meetings. You're welcome to stay with us.'

And there were those eyes again. And that devastating smile. Did he *ever* take his eyes off her?

'I'll have to check my diary, Jack,' she said firmly. 'I have other commitments besides this book; other publishing houses.'

'Please?' asked Connor in the same tone he'd used in the office earlier when asking her to come for dinner. How could she stay angry at him when he was so lovely!

'I should probably get the cover art formally finalised before I go booking trans-Atlantic flights!'

'I have a spare room in my place. You're welcome to stay there, and leave Jack and Jess to have a honeymoon,' he offered boldly.

'Won't your wife mind?' Topaz asked, curtly.

'Connor…' Jack started, but Connor interrupted him.

'My wife won't mind at all. Not one bit. She'd be delighted to meet you,' he insisted. 'So, you'll come?'

The nerve!

'Like I said, I'll need to check my diary.'

The Children's Labyrinth, the most famous bookshop in the world, was almost a New York landmark. No wonder he had such negotiating power with the publisher. If The Labyrinth recommended a book, the author became an overnight sensation. Never mind book reviews or TV chat shows or expensive advertising campaigns, if a children's author wanted fame it came through that shop.

'Well, it's a perfect place for a book launch, that's

for sure,' and she said that wholeheartedly. She'd been there about four times, each time she'd been to New York. *Why hadn't she ever seen Connor there before*, she wondered. Well, it was a huge shop. It wasn't surprising, she thought to herself afterwards.

'Would you like me to do extra illustrations for promos?' she found herself offering. Excitement began to build in her belly. Nerves? Anticipation? Fear? Whatever it was, one thing was for sure: She was going to see Connor Murphy again.

When the evening was over, and they prepared to part ways, Connor reached forward and kissed Topaz on the cheek. 'I very much look forward to seeing you again, Miss Lane.' The words sounded so good coming from him. It reminded her of butter waffles melting in her mouth. He smelt so good, too. She felt completely disarmed. What could she say? Surely he must be able to read that underneath all her protestations she was falling for him, and there was no stopping her.

I do not want to fall for a married man in another country, she told herself. *But*, she wondered, *can you control the heart?*

'Goodbye Connor.' She looked up at him. If only they could keep looking at each other. She didn't want to part, and she most definitely didn't want him to catch a cab to Heathrow. She wanted him to come *home*. To meet Sapphire and Jeff. To meet... *Róisín!* How was Topaz going to keep this a secret?

The Midwife's Cottage

Topaz stepped in her front door when she got back from her train journey and found a note on the table from Sapphire: *Call Róisín. Camira and Jamie are at her house this afternoon, and he'd like to meet up.* She wanted to find out more and to share about Connor, but she could hear Sapphire in the next room in the middle of teaching cello to one of her adult pupils. The haunting strings of Bach's Unaccompanied Cello Suite No. 1 filled the house with a beauty that only music can bring.

'Hi Róisín, it's Topaz. Just got your message from Saph. Are they still at your place?'

'Yes, can you come over?'

'I'll be there in ten minutes. See you.' She hung up the receiver, brushed her hair, and was out the door.

As soon as Topaz met Jamie she should see why Camira had fallen in love with him, and how he was so attuned to her parenting plans. She thought about the beautifully built waterbirth pool, and what a labour of love it had been. *That's the sort of hands-on dad that I'd like for my children,* she thought. And then, Topaz Lane caught herself allowing for the possibility. She'd been so closed off to the idea for so long. "Once bitten, twice shy" had been taken to a whole new level for her. Topaz vowed never to let a man hurt her again. With that, came the reality that without the risk to love there could be no possibility of a love interest. *Everyone on the planet has to take the risk,* her family had told her over and over again.

Jamie poured her a cup of limeflower tea, and

they talked about their birth plans, and how Topaz could assist them, if she was still willing.

'We're having a fairly hands-off birth. Róisín will be there, but mostly to witness,' Jamie explained.

'Like a birth guardian,' Camira added.

'The more people there are in the room, the more likely labour is to slow down or stall. The key thing is to be of support but in a very behind-the-scenes sort of way. Does that make sense at all?' Jamie asked, hoping she'd catch his enthusiasm for natural birth.

'Actually, it reminds me of my cat Matisse when she gave birth to kittens. She wanted to be in the dark, out of the way, but also to know we were there,' Topaz said thoughtfully.

Róisín smiled. 'That's spot on. Women are mammals too, obviously, and the three things we need to give birth naturally and easily are privacy, darkness and quiet.'

'That is like a cat!' Topaz said. 'Well, I can offer you all those things. I'll just think like a cat!'

'There's not usually any reason for a woman not to have pain-free birth. Fear of labour and birth leads to pain. Nature designed a woman to birth easily, in about twenty minutes, and to bend forward and catch her own baby ~ not to have someone pull it away from her,' Róisín said matter-of-factly.

Camira added. 'We're having a lotus birth.'

Topaz looked at her quizzically, as if to say *what the hell is that?*

'It means the baby's cord won't be cut. It will break off naturally a few days later. It's not nearly as gruesome as it sounds. I promise. You see, the longer the cord is left uncut, the better it is for the baby.'

'I didn't know that,' Topaz said.

'And just so you know, I won't be eating my placenta!' Camira reassured her.

'Most vegetarian mammals don't eat their placenta either,' Topaz said, remembering a documentary she once watched.

'We'll be planting it under a tree in the garden,' Jamie said. 'A tree we can see from the family-room window. The idea is for our child to grow up with their tree.'

Róisín joined in. 'In some cultures, the placenta is considered to be the twin or 'grandmother' of the baby.'

Topaz considered this for a few moments, then asked, 'How can I help when the baby's born?'

'Róisín tells us you're a great cook,' Camira smiled. 'Any chance of a pot of soup or something like that so Jamie and I can just stay in bed with the baby for a while? Jamie's taking a month off work so we can have a proper babymoon.'

'What a lovely thing to call it! Well, I'm at your service. I'm almost up to date with all my work projects, so my time is flexible. I'll start planning the menu,' Topaz winked, recognising what an honour it was to be part of this family's journey. 'You know, I don't think most parents give this much thought to the birth or way they'll parent. I imagine it must make the world of difference to be on the same page as your partner, and to be making such conscious choices,' Topaz reflected.

'It does!' Róisín agreed. 'I wish it was written into law that people prepared for parenting the way Camira and Jamie have. What a different world we'd live in.'

The couple said goodbye, and promised to call as soon as labour began. Róisín offered Topaz another cup of tea. 'Connor was so pleased to meet you the other day. I'm sorry we had to rush off.'

'He seems like a lovely man. A shame you didn't bring him to my match-making dinner!' she joked, but inside she was deadly serious. Topaz desperately wanted to tell Róisín that she and Connor had been out to dinner; that he'd kissed her, hugged her; that they were working on a book together. But how could she tell her when Connor wanted to keep it as a surprise? She felt like she was betraying her friend by keeping her in the dark.

'Really?' Róisín smiled. 'It was such a surprise visit, but even though it was brief I'm so glad he was able to come and see me. I miss him terribly, but you know I'm so pleased that he was able to make himself a life elsewhere. He grew up an only child, and he really deserved to have brothers and sisters. Don't get me wrong, I didn't neglect him. He was dearly loved and nurtured, but I'm acutely aware that he grew up in the shadow of a dead sister, and that's not easy for any child. A mother's grief isn't something you can lock in a box and pretend isn't there. It shows up when you least expect it. You might think it's just on birthdays or anniversaries, but it can happen when you hear a piece of music in a shop or a friend loses someone they love. Even the wind blowing the wrong way can take you right back to the beginning. Suddenly you feel like you're in the thick of grief all over again. It never really leaves you. But you know this, don't you Topaz?'

'Yes, I do,' she said, and was quiet for a few moments. 'I find it so painful to see mothers with their babies. It's excruciating for me when I see a mum half pulling her child's arm out of the socket or shaming him in public. I just want to yell "Don't you know how lucky you are!" But, of course, I keep my mouth shut. It's a daily pain, and it feels like such hard work sometimes. Did having Connor help? Did it ease the pain?'

'Loving Connor has been a healing balm. No other child can take away the pain and grief, but what it does do is allow you to grow your heart. And that's the whole point of being a mother anyway: To grow your heart. What I have learnt though is that you can love other people's children, say through adoption or friends' children, and still grow your heart as equally and as fully as if you birthed a child. Mothering begins in the heart. Once you start on that path, it never ends.

When my husband died, I really thought my world might end. He was my soulmate…the one who got me through Eden's death. The silent shoulder, always there. I knew that Connor had to break free or he'd have no life at all. He was just eighteen years old. A dear penfriend of mine in the USA invited him over for a visit. Connor fell in love with the place, and with a girl, and made a really good friend in Simon. Together they started a small bookshop, but then when their partnership broke up Connor took over and kept expanding the store. It was like he'd found his passion in life. He did a degree in children's literature, part-time, while running his bookshop. I often wonder if his passion for children's books came about partly as a result of a childhood deprived of siblings. He always had friends, but just a select few. Connor's not the sort of person to have people around as decorations. If someone's in his life, it's because they really mean something to him. He's the person you want watching your back. And he's great with kids! I've been to a couple of book launches at his shop and he's like the Pied Piper, minus the flute. Children get a real sense that he's genuine. Kids aren't stupid, they know when adults are authentic.'

Topaz caught her breath. How could it be that Róisín knew her son so well when they lived in different countries and had been apart for so long? 'He sounds like a very special man,' she said.

'It was good and right that he moved away when he did. And good for me, too. I was able to grieve deeply for my husband in a way that felt right to me...and I didn't have to hide my feelings for fear of upsetting him. Connor had his own grief, of course, and he was deeply upset by his father's death. They'd been best mates. That's a deep loss to bear when you're on the verge of manhood and your friend and mentor is suddenly gone. Connor actually lost both parents at that time, in a way. I disappeared into a world that took me about two years to emerge from. But you know, despite the distance, we're as close as possible. Anyway, enough about my boy.'

Topaz left, having said she looked forward to seeing Róisín again at Camira's birth. She couldn't sleep that night, and took a stroll in the garden. Sitting under the light of a waning full Moon, her thoughts drifted to Connor. Again. He'd been through greater losses than she had, but he had a smile to light the whole world. How had he moved on with his life in such a powerful way? How had she stayed so stuck?

Love Never dies

Roisin, aged 46

'Can I get you some more water, my love?' she tenderly asked her dying husband. Frail and weak, his lips were dry; his mouth parched, and his eyes were closed. The rattle drum of pneumonia hummed inside his weak chest like a menacing teenage boy racer. It was a secondary infection caused by an aggressive bacterium which defied medical treatment.

Róisín held his white hand, and gently sang him his favourite Irish song as he drifted unconscious again. It was just a matter of time now until death would come knocking. There was no point fighting it. She had no control over whether he lived or died. That was the Breathmaker's choice. Her husband's choice had been to die at home. He didn't want to be in hospital, either for himself or for Róisín and her memories of Eden.

Outside the wooden sash window of their Irish farm cottage, sharing the late-afternoon sky with the setting Sun, were thousands upon thousands of starlings in the dance of murmuration. Small black bodies stencilled a monochrome kaleidoscope of flying this way and that, thousands of birds changing direction at once, in and over the flock. In her heart, she set the image to Pachelbel's Canon in D major. Róisín would never forget this day. The birds were going this way and that: back, forwards, sideways. Acrobatic genius, at every turn of the wing. So much life, it seemed, and yet Róisín could see and feel death everywhere around her, too, not just in the Autumn leaves drifting by the bedroom window. Were the birds giving her a message? Even if just to say: that, no matter what, life goes on. It always keeps moving forward. Yes, even after the death of someone we love dearly.

Her hope, her trust, her confidence, her enthusiasm, her dreams; she felt that they were all dying right there beside the love of her life. Róisín had been down the road of death before. Back then, more than twenty years ago, it had come suddenly with no warning. It had cruelly stalked her in the night. 'There! We've got your baby!' it screeched like a demon from hell to her agonised heart, the memory still taunting her decades later.

This death gave her time, even if only for a few weeks. Time was letting her say goodbye. Time was being kind to her, though she often wondered if that was true. To say goodbye to a baby who doesn't even get the chance to see the world is the cruellest death. It is the death of possibility, and very few can fully understand the depth of that unless they too have walked in those shoes. Parents are not meant to outlive their children, or so we're told.

But what of the death of someone you've known most of your life? The person who knows everything about you, and can read your thoughts and pre-empt your needs? Isn't that death just as cruel? Is it less painful because you've had all those years of possibility manifest into fruition? Róisín couldn't decide. Loss was loss no matter what way you labelled it.

And then the birds flew off. She sat quietly; Connor's head hung low, as he wept softly on the other side of his father's bed.

And there it was: breathing had ceased. He was gone. 'Goodbye my love.' And her soft and silent tears said the rest. In the still of the afternoon, she let the fading sunlight disappear beyond the horizon with the birds. She hugged her son, slowly, for the longest time. Their sobs of pain, loss and grief, united. And then they returned to their chairs in silence.

Under a full Moon in October, Róisín let the old rocking chair ~ where she'd once breastfed Connor in childhood ~ and her late mother's old crocheted blanket, hold her as the tears fell. There was no need for emergency calls to anyone. Later, she would pick up the phone and call her friends.

Róisín sat in the silence, feeling the embrace of her soul's love as she held his hand and thanked him for all the memories. He was gone from his body, but he was still there, energetically, in the bedroom, loving them more than he had ever done. Somehow, he wasn't quite gone.

Eventually, mother and son crawled into bed beside the body of the man who had brought so much love and laughter into their lives.

Two days later, after visits from friends and family paying their last respects and prayers, Kevin Murphy, wearing just a cloth shroud, was laid to rest beneath the old oak tree in the garden. Buried near the rope swing he'd pushed his son on over and over, he kept company beneath the damp, dark soil with the remains of more than a dozen cats, an Irish setter, a raven, and a few rusty toy Matchbox cars.

A couple of months later, Connor travelled to New York to stay with friends. Six months after that, when it looked like he would be staying on, Róisín rented out the cottage to a young cousin, and moved to rural Cumbria. In deliberate solitude, she spent the next two years growing a medicinal herb garden, making teas and tinctures for when she was ready to begin midwifery again. A time of solitude, rest and introspection, she found herself being nurtured by soil and sunshine. Róisín used this sabbatical to write in a journal, study her dreams, listen to the world's most beautiful music, rescue stray cats from the animal refuge centre, and grow herbs. She was saying goodbye to her life as the wife of a good man, and that wasn't easy. But eventually the day did come when she knew it was time to 'be with woman' again.

The Blessed Way

Sapphire opened the green envelope, and read the invitation out loud.

Topaz and Sapphire
are invited to Camira's blessingway ceremony
in honour of the new life she's creating.

When the afternoon of the blessingway ceremony arrived, Topaz checked her list to make sure she had everything she wanted to bring along: A slice of wood from a silver birch branch, with a hole drilled through it, to give as a blessing bead; some starflowers that had fallen to the ground in the vegetable beds; a lavender-scented beeswax candle; and a poem about children. She also packed a bag filled with dried fennel seeds to use for nursing tea. And, of course, way too much food to share afterwards!

Róisín greeted them in Camira's garden. 'Hi ladies. Welcome. Make yourself comfortable in the yurt on a cushion. Camira will join us once everyone's arrived.' Topaz reached over for a hug. 'Thank you so much for inviting both of us.'

They took their places and smiled at the five other women who were already in there. Two more women arrived. A CD filled the space with beautiful music. Topaz closed her eyes to Nana Mouskouri singing Schubert's *Serenade*.

When the blessingway was about to begin, Topaz was surprised that Róisín wasn't leading the ceremony. A woman, who Topaz didn't know, stood up to speak.

'Good afternoon. Thank you for forming

this sacred circle. My name's Miranda, and I'm the celebrant for today's blessingway ceremony.' In her early fifties, she was slim, with shoulder-length wavy brown hair. She wore a white, long, velvet dress, and had bare feet. At the door of the yurt, Miranda rang a bell three times, announcing to Camira that they were ready for her to join them.

The yurt smelled of rose incense; and beeswax tea-light candles formed a circle in the centre of the space. A small wood-burning stove took the edge off the Autumn chill. Topaz looked at the song sheet Róisín had included with the blessingway invitation and smiled at the lyrics.

Camira arrived, and gently bowed her head in respect before entering the yurt. She was in awe to see how Róisín and Miranda had prepared the circle space of this Mongolian tent. Afternoon sunlight filtered through the canvas, and then through red, purple and pink saris, which created the feel of a woman's womb. Soft, large, red cushions and cotton rugs provided comfort and softness. Camira seated herself on a chair that had been decorated with red ribbons and flowers.

With the gentleness of a deer in a pine forest, Miranda walked gracefully around the circle, wafting burning sage. 'This is our sacred medicine wheel,' she affirmed. 'In the Navajo tradition, let us give thanks.' She breathed in gently for a few moments.

'The blessingway ceremony is as old as the Navajo Indians, and as young as the baby here in utero. Today we affirm that Camira is to have a beautiful, ecstatic birth experience. That is our wish.'

Miranda cast the circle, and breathed in deeply. 'We meet in this sacred space to witness Camira on her journey into motherhood.'

This was no baby shower! Topaz thought about what it must be like to be nurtured in this way.

Why would anyone not want this during her eighth month of pregnancy? To be surrounded by the beauty and purity of angels, invisible ancestors and love was surely the most beautiful gift to bestow.

Miranda told the circle of women that the birthing candle which she was about to light was to symbolically call in the ancient mothers.

'I will begin, and then ask each of you to introduce yourselves in the same way. My name is Miranda, and I'm the daughter of Marie, granddaughter of Kelly and Janice.'

Topaz listened carefully as the women introduced themselves and their ancestresses. When she heard Sapphire say their mother's name and their grandmothers' names, she felt a bond that stretched through time, not just with her blood sister, but with all women. *We are all daughters*, she thought to herself.

'My name is Topaz, and I'm the daughter of Anastasia and the granddaughter of Liselle and Louise.' Tears trickled down her cheeks. She wasn't embarrassed by this. Naming their foremothers had triggered high emotion in every woman here. Even Miranda, the celebrant, had choked a little. When the introductions were finished, they joined in song to sing *Ancient Mother*.

'Birth is a spiritual vision quest,' Miranda told the circle. 'It unites the mother-to-be with all women in her chosen community. The beads we gift Camira today are one more bead on a long strand which connects all mothers and daughters across time and space.'

'Camira, I give you this bead,' offered Topaz. 'It's made from the wood of a silver birch tree, from

106

the woodland at the back of my garden. I give you this bead to connect you to Mother Earth.'

Camira grabbed her hands. They were fast becoming good friends, and had felt that from the moment they met. All the women in the circle presented Camira with a blessingway bead.

'Róisín will now come forward, and, as a midwife, will wash Camira's feet with herbal water. The role of a midwife is a humble one. Afterwards, we will all take turns to brush Camira's hair. The ritual brushing will lead us to change her hairstyle as a symbol of the changes about to take place in her life,' said Miranda.

The circle closed with another song, and Miranda thanked the ancient mothers and other unseen guests for joining them.

'May this circle be open, but unbroken. Go in peace. We will now join together for supper,' Miranda said.

Róisín, Topaz and Sapphire went to the kitchen and brought back trays of food and drinks for the women to enjoy. This was a day that none of them would ever forget.

Torn Apart

Camira at 16

'You're *what*?' screeched Camira's furious mother. 'Pregnant? How did that happen?'

Camira would have smiled at her mother's lack of awareness for human biology, except for the fact she was terrified at the anger being hurled in her direction.

'You've brought shame on this family. I'm so disgusted! We're seeing the doctor first thing tomorrow,' and with that she slammed the door, leaving Camira and her father alone in the room.

Her father didn't say anything. He didn't scold her, but neither did he comfort her. Camira's father was one of those brow-beaten men who did as his wife said. Camira could see in his kind eyes that he wasn't happy with how his wife had just acted, but he didn't have the emotional strength to speak up. In that moment, Camira *hated* him! She hated his cowardice, and vowed never to marry a spineless man who couldn't protect her. His complete lack of gumption was as repulsive to Camira as her mother's controlling nature.

At ten minutes to nine in the morning, Camira's mother drove her to the doctor's surgery. 'We have to dispose of this problem,' she told the doctor firmly, not leaving room for discussion. 'She's not keeping it,' the mother said in a cold way that sounded as if Camira had been impregnated with the sperm of the Devil himself.

'Noooooo!' Camira cried. 'This is *my* baby, not yours. I'm not killing it!'

'I'm sorry, but you're my child, under *my* roof. You will do as I say.'

Camira could hear the doctor gulp, and in that moment she realised there probably wasn't a man on the planet who'd speak up to her mother. There was no-one to protect her or her baby. She was alone.

'I'll contact the clinic and make an appointment for the procedure,' he said dutifully, avoiding all eye contact with Camira.

'You are NOT killing my baby, mother!' she yelled, tears rushing down her red, blotchy face.

'How are you going to raise this baby? How are you going to put a roof over its head? *I'm* not doing it! No, Camira. It's settled. You're not ready to be a mother. You've no idea what it involves,' she spat. 'Don't argue with me. I'm your mother.'

Camira sobbed all the way home, and for the next week leading up to and beyond the termination.

On the day she would never, ever forget, the nurse was very kind to her. The anaesthetist, too, showed empathy by gently touching her hand longer than perhaps he should have. As Camira came out of anaesthetic, she wept softly into the pillow. 'Where's my baby?' she cried to the nurse. 'I want my baby.' The words and her sobbing echoed through the recovery ward. She cried for her lost baby, and for herself. Never would she let anyone tell her how to run her body again. Camira left that day a different person. Estranged from both her parents, she barely passed a word over the next two years. Biding her time until she was able to be considered an adult, she kept to herself and secretly planned a future of freedom.

'Mother, I will never forgive you.' They were the last words Camira said to her mother when she left home on her 18th birthday. Leaving her past behind her, she began work at an interior-decorating business as an assistant. 'You'll never know just how cruel you were, will you?'

Camira fell head over heels in love with Jamie when she was twenty two. They started for a family straight away, but for the next twenty three years, pregnancy eluded her. Their love carried them through dark and desperate times, but it never wavered. Their love and devotion to each other was absolute with or without children.

It wasn't pregnancy that brought Camira to Róisín's front door, but the claggy, relentless, vice-like grip of infertility. Extensive tests revealed that neither Jamie nor Camira had problems physically with their fertility. Many couples would have been worn down by two decades of regular menstrual cycles. It was by chance that Camira saw a feature article in the local paper about a shamanic midwife who worked with women to help them overcome psychological infertility.

'Jamie, do you think that's what I've got? Psychological infertility?' she asked him one night after their tender lovemaking.

'Honey,' he whispered, stroking her back gently, 'what your mother made you do was horrible and inexcusable. I don't doubt that deep inside you're scared to be pregnant. I know you desperately want a baby, but if there's a part of you that's terrified of hearing your mother's voice and her total condemnation, then yeah, it's highly likely that it's psychological. But you know, you mustn't think that it means there's something wrong with you. Look at it as a protection mechanism. I do think, though,' he hesitated for a moment, unsure of how she's react, 'that at some point you need to forgive your mother, as hard as that might be.'

Camira sighed. She realised Jamie was probably right.

He held her close. 'Honey, your body is wise. It always has been, at least as long as I've known you. You know your body really well. You know your cycles, when you're ovulating, and when you are your most creative. You take a sabbatical during your period, and seek solitude. You know yourself inside out. Maybe it's time to look at the whole issue with your mum, and the baby who died, on a much deeper level,' he said, kissing her on the cheek.

'Jamie, it feels huge. Whenever I've thought about that time of my life, it's just been too overwhelming. I've purposely tried not to think about it too much,' Camira admitted.

'But sweetheart, if that's what's standing between us having a baby, then let's deal with it. I have no doubt that you're going to be a great mother, and if that's through adoption then that's fine with me. But why not contact this lady? You've got nothing to lose.'

Róisín worked one-on-one with Camira for several months. They looked at dietary and homeopathic remedies to open her, in mind, body and soul. They began dream therapy, and non-dominant handwriting, journaling, and divination cards to channel her inner child. Mostly, Róisín acted in her true capacity as a midwife: *she listened*. They made connections between how Camira was mothered, and how she wanted to mother. Love and fear, trust and mistrust. No psychological stone was left unturned. At times, the depth felt harrowing, but Camira instinctively knew she was on the path to recovering her fertility.

And then one day, Camira realised her period had been due a few days before. Most women wouldn't have thought twice, but Camira's body ran like clockwork to the Moon's cycle. 'Can it be?' she dared to ask herself, when she also noticed that she was peeing more often, and her breasts felt a little tender.

Jamie and Camira turned up unannounced on Róisín's doorstep, with swollen, red eyes. 'Whatever is the matter?' she asked, inviting them in.

'We're pregnant!' Camira couldn't say it quickly enough. 'We're having a baby! Will you be our midwife?'

Birth Becomes Her

The big hand had just gone ten o'clock. Topaz was tidying around the white porcelain kitchen sink when the phone rang. She knew immediately that it was Camira or Jamie, as the phone never rang beyond 8pm.

She'd spent the day pottering around the kitchen, making soup: carrot and ginger, minestrone, Goan potato and spinach, Moroccan chickpea and apricot, lentil and lemon. There were soups for each day for a fortnight, all ready to go into Camira's freezer. Assorted casseroles and stews made from lentils, and beans and vegetables from the garden, were sitting in rows on the kitchen table. Topaz had also made some containers of cooked brown basmati rice, seasoned quinoa, and gently spiced couscous. She smiled, and had to admit to herself that she got a bit carried away.

Birth food, she told herself. And she felt great. *This is what a family needs to feel nurtured. A personal chef!*

She'd had several conversations and walks through Róisín's herb garden to know just what would nourish Camira after the birth. Bags of nettle tea for iron, raspberry leaf tea to help her uterus back into shape, and chamomile for relaxation. The dried leaves were labelled, and placed into a wicker basket.

'Hello, Topaz speaking.'

'Hey Topaz, it's Jamie. Our baby is on the way,' he said excitedly.

Topaz couldn't help the tears. What joy! What a precious moment in anyone's life.

'I'm on my way.'

When Topaz arrived ten minutes later, she saw that Róisín was already there. As she quietly let herself into the house, gentle moaning noises greeted her. At first, she thought she'd overheard Jamie and Camira making love. These were the sounds of *pleasure,* and not at all what people associated with the trauma of having a baby.

Róisín was in the front room, knitting. 'Come and join me,' she beckoned. 'Camira doesn't need us right now. You can hear from the sounds she's making that everything is just wonderful.'

'Those sounds...I....' she didn't need to continue. Róisín knew exactly what she was thinking. Smiling, she agreed: 'A midwife's dream! A woman in ecstasy. This is a pleasurable birth. You could call it orgasmic. Camira is a woman who is mentally and emotionally ready for birth, with a partner by her side. Neither of them has any fear. This is how birth was meant to be,' Róisín whispered.

'This is not what they showed us in school!' Topaz whispered back.

Róisín said, 'I know! I'm sure those images are designed as teenage contraception!' They both giggled softly into the night air.

'We'll go in a little later, if they want us in, but for now my job is to sit on my hands, metaphorically. I'm going to keep knitting! My job is to see, in my mind, that baby being born easily and beautifully. As a midwife, that's the most important part of my job.'

Topaz closed her eyes, and she too imagined Camira continuing to emit the moans of a woman being pleasured. She found the idea of birthing in this way rather erotic, and felt the enormous intimacy of the occasion, and then Topaz wondered why any couple would choose to have others in the birthing room during labour, especially strangers. Wondering if this was birth's best-kept secret, she asked herself: *Is this why women are told it's dangerous and painful? To scare us into submission? Are women culturally hypnotised into believing it will hurt, so that, in fact, we don't have millions of women around the world giving birth in orgasmic pleasure?* She didn't allow herself to become annoyed at the possibility, but instead turned her thoughts to imagining this baby easing its way down the birth canal, gently, smoothly, easily.

'You're birthing beautifully, my darling,' she heard Jamie say encouragingly and with pride. Topaz smiled. For a moment she thought of Andy. Would he have supported her in birth this way? It was hard to even picture him in a good light now, and she thanked God for unanswered prayers. That shocked her right back into her body. For the first time in years she was actually grateful that they were no longer together. Was there something in the magic of this home tonight that made her aware that she'd had a lucky escape?

Róisín whispered, 'The baby's almost here.'

Topaz became aware that the gentle moaning had stopped. 'How do you know?'

'She's in transition. The expansions which lead baby down the birth canal have eased. The intensity has gone, and now her body will naturally push the baby out. There's no need for anyone, least of all a midwife, to tell a woman to push. The body does this of its own accord.'

Topaz noticed the midwifery bag half-open: calendula cream, motherwort tincture, hot-water bottle, coconut oil, essential oil of lavender, pinard, scissors, needle, cotton, fabrics, and herbs to release the placenta: basil, nutmeg, and honey.

Jamie's head appeared at the doorway. 'Would you like to see our baby being born?' he beamed.

Topaz and Róisín tiptoed into the birthing room. Topaz was taken aback at its magical transformation. She felt as if she'd entered another world. The bedroom had become a birth oasis, lit only with beeswax candles, but there was enough light to see.

Jasmine scent lingered in the air. Mozart's music played softly in the background. Topaz had created a birthing compilation of his gentlest pieces. That Camira was playing it caught Topaz right in the heart. Her favourite music, here, at this birth. How blessed for a child to arrive Earthside to the sound of one of the world's most gifted composers.

The bedroom was filled with large vases of fresh, red, Autumn lilies. A small table was set up by the birthing pool, and had pictures and items which were obviously important to Camira: a painting of a beautiful mother; baby booties; a photo of a woman birthing in water; affirmations which said things like: *Birth is beautiful. I love giving birth. My baby is safe. I catch my baby easily.* There were crystals and flowers, too.

Around Camira's neck was the necklace she'd threaded during labour. Made from the beads of all the women at her blessingway ceremony, it shone in the candlelight. The women of Camira's community had each given their blessing for this birth, and although most of them were now in bed asleep, at the most profound level they were here with her, now, as she felt her vagina stretching easily, opening, yielding. Round like a sunflower fully in bloom! *Open, open, open.*

Topaz remembered their conversation about the mammalian needs of a woman in birth: quiet, privacy and darkness. These were absolutely essential. And Róisín's words about the importance of not making eye contact with a woman in labour came back to her, too. *All these things stimulate the neocortex*, Róisín had said. *That's the front part of the brain. We don't want that. In birth, a woman needs to be in her reptilian brain.*

Camira had been in labour for about an hour, and now her baby was ready to be born. Topaz and Róisín were squatting quietly either side of the pool. Jamie was behind Camira, gently supporting her. Topaz could see the head of the baby in-between Camira's legs. The beauty of the moment overwhelmed her. Tears nestled into the corner of her eyes. There was no comparison between this and the woman in stirrups screaming during birth on the video shown in high school. No comparison at all.

Newborn baby hair gently waved in the water. This was an exquisite moment, and Topaz recognised that as she felt everything in slow motion.

'You're amazing,' Topaz whispered to Camira, but was barely audible.

Camira smiled, and with that the rest of the baby's body rushed forward into the warm water. She gently reached in front of her, and lifted the slippery newborn up into her arms. Jamie was crying with joy. 'We have our baby!' he said over and over like a man who'd lost his mind.

Time of birth: 11.04pm.

Róisín unobtrusively checked the baby over for colour and vigour. The infant wasn't crying, but calm and relaxed.

Camira looked between her baby's legs. 'We have a girl!' She started crying with joy. The emotion and magnificence of the evening lingered like exotic perfume. Topaz and Róisín topped the pool up with some more warm water. Jamie kept kissing Camira, and saying how amazing she was.

'You are a Goddess. You were incredible.' His ecstasy was infectious.

The placenta was birthed ten minutes later, without fuss. Róisín had already advised Camira that in the event of it not coming out, they would try some midwifery tricks, such as herbs or blowing on an empty bottle. The latter worked without fail, in Róisín's experience.

Topaz tiptoed back to the kitchen and prepared a tray with a pot of raspberry leaf tea. She added a bit of raw wildflower honey, knowing it would nourish the new mother, and that the tea would tighten her uterus. When she arrived back in the bedroom, Róisín was helping the new family get into the family bed. She put the placenta into a sieve inside a large bowl so it could drain any excess blood at the start of their lotus birth.

Topaz was intrigued with the pulsing life-force of the baby's cord and dinner-plate-sized placenta before her. Round, like mandala art, this vibrant organ, fresh from the mysteries of the womb, invited the strong umbilical cord into its centre, where it forged its identity as a trunk reaching up to an assortment of blood vessels imitating the branches of a mature tree. *It's a work of art*, she thought to herself. And in that moment, she knew that she would have to paint a placenta. *Why was this considered hospital waste*, she wondered, when all she could see was beauty. The tree of life etched by its very veins. The colours were rich: indigo, burgundy, pearl, crimson.

Róisín felt Camira's soft belly. With the baby now born, it gave way to her hands like ricotta cheese:

soft and spongy. Feeling to see if the womb was tightening, she came away happy. Beneath the loose, floppy, stretch-marked skin, it felt firm.

When they were all in bed, with the baby in the middle, Camira helped to latch her new child onto the breast. Topaz was in awe. This new little creature, fresh into the world, puckered its lips and instinctively knew what to do.

The new mother's eyes were fixed firmly on her new child. Nestled softly against her mother's yielding breasts, the infant girl began her work of suckling. Camira's breasts wept with happiness: creamy droplets of colostrum dropping into the arch of the infant's mouth.

'That is one hungry little girl!' Jamie laughed. He had his hand on Camira's hand.

If ever there was a love story, Topaz mused. She didn't feel jealous though, she felt joy. And hope!

Settling the tray on the bedside table, Topaz poured them each a cup of steaming tea.

'I've brought food for the freezer,' she whispered, not wanting to disturb the ambience. 'I'll put it in now, and then come back in the morning to see if there's anything I can do. I'm so incredibly proud of you all, and so, so happy,' she said, her voice breaking with emotion. 'I feel like I've just given birth myself. Thank you,' she sniffed. 'Sleep well.'

'Thank you for being here. It means so much to us,' Camira said.

'I'll be back first thing as well,' Róisín added. 'That's a very healthy and beautiful baby girl you have there. Good night.'

After Topaz unpacked the food for the freezer, she walked outside in the dark of the night to her car. Standing under the stars, she breathed in deeply. *This is the meaning of life*, she thought to herself: *love and beauty*. 'I've just witnessed one of life's miracles,' she said softly to Róisín, who'd waited outside for her.

'You have indeed. Extraordinary, yet ordinary all at the same time. Birth is happening all over the world right now.'

'Yes, but how many of those births will be like this one?' Topaz asked, but she knew the answer.

'Not many, but I have faith that as more women, like Camira, take back their power and birth naturally and joyfully, word will get out,' she laughed. 'Women need to let go of the badge of honour around difficult births and to grant themselves the right to birth instinctively. Our ancestresses knew the secrets of ecstatic birthing. It's in our blood. I can't help but wonder if women think they're betraying the sisterhood by *not* having a difficult birth,' she added thoughtfully. 'Go and get some sleep, Topaz.'

They hugged each other goodnight. It was a long, slow, rocking hug, witnessed only by the stars, and Topaz felt the tears come up again. That salt water wasn't going to stay inside. 'I'm sorry,' she said.

'Don't ever apologise for feeling, Topaz. Tears are shed in sadness and happiness. They're the river of life. Let it flow. I'm so glad you were able to see Camira's birth. This evening will never leave your memory. You've been imprinted with ecstatic birth and will take that with you throughout life, and you'll be able to pass it on to the next generation.'

'If I have children,' she replied solemnly, head hanging down.

'Oh, you will,' Róisín added confidently.

Lavender and Joy

In the morning, Topaz grabbed a large bag of dried lavender flowers that she'd harvested the Summer before. Camira had asked her if she had any spare as it would be helpful for their lotus birth.

As she arrived at Camira's front door, Topaz saw that Jamie had left it ajar so she could enter freely. Róisín was already in the bedroom, affirming that Camira and baby were thriving.

'Good morning,' Topaz said softly. 'Your baby is so beautiful,' she smiled.

Camira and Jamie prepared the placenta following Róisín's guidance by sprinkling it with salt and dried lavender flowers. Róisín reached into her midwifery bag and grabbed the essential oil of lavender, and sprinkled a few drops on it too.

Topaz enjoyed the company of the new family for about half an hour, then asked, 'Is there anything I can do for you before I go?'

'Jamie put a load of washing on earlier. Would you mind hanging it on the line?' Camira asked, unsure if she was asking something beyond the norm.

'Of course I can. And what a great drying day, too. I'll put some soup on the stove, and Jamie can heat it up at lunchtime when you're ready.'

Topaz stood in the morning sunshine of Autumn, hanging up this new family's laundry, and marvelling at how such a simple household chore could be so pleasurable. Hanging washing up outside had always been her favourite housekeeping job, but today it was exquisite. Sacred housekeeping.

121

Topaz returned each morning, and on the fourth day saw for herself that the cord had broken naturally. Their baby had been lotus born, as had been Camira and Jamie's wish.

'Tomorrow we'll go in the garden and plant the placenta under the tree. Would you like to be here when we do that?' Jamie asked, hoping Topaz would say yes.

'I'd be delighted.' Topaz headed to the kitchen, sliced up some of the sourdough bread she'd baked early that morning, and took a container of lentil and tomato soup from the freezer. She was thoroughly enjoying her new routine: starting the day with visits to Camira and Jamie's house, then heading back to her art studio mid-morning to work on the Mosaic cover illustration. It was almost complete.

Topaz decided to put some washing on, and swept Camira's kitchen floor. Once the washing was done, she hung it on the line to dry. She picked some fresh flowers from the garden and placed them on the dining table, next to the bread. Taking a piece of paper from her handbag, she left a note: Dearest Camira, Jamie and Baby ~ thank you for everything.

The Pear Tree

Róisín, Topaz, Camira and Jamie were in the garden. Camira had just finished breastfeeding the baby, who was now asleep in the sling. 'Shall we do this now?' Jamie asked.

Róisín smiled, and took the container with the placenta. Jamie had already dug a hole in the lawn in a clear part of the garden. She stood reverently by the place where a pear tree would be planted above the placenta. 'On this day, we gather to thank the placenta which nourished this young baby's life for nine months. From the Earth it came, and to the Earth it returns. This child has come to us through the miracle of incarnation. She has come from the Infinite; from that place of mystery that is beyond our human understanding.'

Róisín continued to speak without a script, the words flowing from deep within. Her words eased their way into the deepest part of Topaz's soul.

'Our children's hearts beat with the rhythm of the Universe. Our name forms part of our identity, and today we are celebrating the sacredness of this baby. Our name is a group of sounds, but the vibrations are held together in a unique way. And every time that name is written or spoken, power moves throughout that person's spirit. It stirs within them the unique purpose of their life and the potential within them. We recognise that such a purpose is given to us before birth by the Great Creative Mother. Our divine purpose and destiny are something we define while in this world. Our name,' Róisín reminded them, 'is a powerful indicator of this function, and is sacred. Every time our name is spoken or written it aligns us to our Divine Nature. The naming of a child ritually joins her to her spirit.'

Jamie spontaneously followed her. 'On this day, we dedicate this tree to grow up alongside our daughter, being nourished by the placenta.'

Camira added, with her voice breaking, 'On this day, we name our daughter *Lavender Joy*.'

Róisín wiped her moist tears with a tissue, and then continued. 'Dear Lavender, with a flower and water ~ ancient symbols of beauty and purity ~ I touch your brow, lips and hands to dedicate your thoughts, speech and your deeds to that which is noble and true. May your heart always know love. We pray that your mind always searches for the abundant truth and beauty of this world, and we ask that your eyes always seek justice. May your hands find right livelihood to fulfil you, and may your beautiful body carry you far.'

Jamie placed the placenta in the ground, and then shovelled some dirt on top of it before planting the tree.

'Blessed be,' Róisín said.

'Blessed be,' the other three said in unison.

'Lavender Joy, may all your days be filled with love, and the laughter of friends and family,' Topaz found herself adding, spontaneously.

'Love and laughter,' Róisín repeated after her.

Topaz kept up her post-natal morning visits for more than a month, and as time went on she saw Camira and Jamie emerge into early December from their babymoon bubble a little bit more.

A great bond had developed between them, and their friendship blossomed beautifully. Topaz valued how much she learnt about natural babycare, such as

124

using only natural products on the baby's skin, and keeping her away from electromagnetic radiation, like computers, mobiles and cordless phones. Topaz learnt about breastfeeding, mostly by observing. Sometimes she wore Lavender in a sling while Camira had a shower. Once Jamie was back at work, Topaz and Camira went out walking together most mornings, taking turns to carry Lavender.

The Children's Labyrinth

'Topaz, hi. It's Jacqueline. Jack and Jess aren't going to be able to fly in till later. They're sorry they can't meet you at the airport. Jack said to get a cab straight to The Children's Labyrinth, and Connor will look after you till they arrive,' Jacqueline said as quickly as she could.

'Oh,' Topaz said slowly. 'Oh,' she repeated until Jacqueline replied.

'Connor will look after you, you know. You'll be fine,' she said, reassuringly.

'Yes, I know that,' Topaz agreed. 'My flight arrives at JFK about 2.30pm. Maybe I should just wait there until the end of the day so I don't disturb him at work,' she suggested thoughtfully.

'Are you kidding? Connor is dying to see you again. I'm surprised he's not at Heathrow waiting to escort you himself!' Jacqueline laughed.

'Really? *Really?* How do you know that?' Topaz demanded.

'Never you mind! Just get on that plane and have a fabulous time. You know, you should just stay there for Christmas. I'm sure you could have a couple of weeks off work. There are no great deadlines looming,' she said.

'Going now. I'm going now Jacqueline. Stop talking!' she laughed, and hung up.

Flight 345 Heathrow to JFK boarding now from gate five. Passengers for New York on flight 345 please go to gate five for boarding, came a soothing female voice over the sound system.

126

Topaz felt a flutter in her heart. Was he really looking forward to seeing her again? She thought about that night in the restaurant and how he pleaded with her to come to New York for the book launch. Suddenly she felt like she was fifteen years old again. Bright pink flooded her cheeks. 'Don't be stupid,' she said out loud.

Carrying an overnight bag, she proceeded to board the plane. Seat 5A. She made herself comfortable and was seated next to a frail lady. This suited her perfectly. A companion who'd probably sleep most of the way and leave her to own her thoughts. And what would she be thinking? The same thoughts she'd had since the day she saw Connor Murphy walking through her small market town with Róisín. The same thoughts that kept her awake at night, wondering... wondering, what if?

Closing her eyes, his face came easily. She didn't even need to do that most of the time. His face was there before her. Those twinkling eyes that told the world he loved to laugh, and were always ready with a good joke. Eyes that looked right through her; that spoke to her soul and said *I know you.*

Connor had short, dark-brown hair, with traces of silver and grey, and was in his mid-forties. His dimples always made her smile inside. There was something of the naughty schoolboy about him. *Could you take a man like Connor Murphy seriously?* she wondered. *Or was he just a good-time boy? A ladies' man capable of having any woman he wanted?*

The plane had a bumpy landing, and Topaz felt her stomach turn over. She realised it was probably less about the vulnerability of hitting New York soil so ungracefully than the thought of getting a cab through nightmare traffic, and then finding Connor at The Labyrinth. It was a huge store, and she knew it would probably take several minutes to track him down.

Stepping through the arrivals' gate, she made a mental note of which direction to go for the cabs.

'Topaz,' came the familiar soft Irish lilt from her left.

'Connor,' she gasped, feeling rather foolish. 'What are you doing here? I, I....'

'I wasn't going to let you fight your way through New York on your own. Hug?' he asked, but his smile made it perfectly clear that he wasn't going to wait for her permission. He picked her up and twirled her around. 'It's so good to see you again.'

She didn't resist. It felt good. Safe. He held her like there was no tomorrow. He smelt good. *What is that scent?* she wondered. It was the same one as when they'd met for dinner in London.

Eventually he pulled away. 'You look amazing,' he said, taking her in.

'After a seven-and-a-half-hour flight? You're joking, right?' she laughed.

'Not at all.' Connor took her bag. 'Is this all you've got?'

'Yes.'

'Not staying long then?' he asked, not hiding his disappointment.

'Just a couple of nights...I don't want to outstay my welcome. Your wife might not like me...' she said, realising she'd not even given that woman any thought for some time.

Connor sighed, and said, 'Follow me.' They got into a cab, and headed to The Labyrinth. 'I'll take you through the bookshop later. First we'll head home, and you can freshen up and we can have a drink,' he said, matter-of-factly. His tone had definitely changed since she mentioned 'the wife'.

His apartment was at the top of the bookshop, an old converted warehouse, with expansive views over the city and Hudson River. Topaz immediately felt at home. It was more like a jungle than a house, filled with so many lush tropical plants. She was surprised, though, how masculine it felt, with maroons and other autumnal colours in the décor.

'This is your room,' he said, showing her a simply decorated room with handmade, oak furniture. 'The bathroom is over there. Towels are in the wardrobe. If there's anything else you need, just ask. I'll put the kettle on.'

'Connor, have I upset you somehow? It's just that...'

'I'm not married, Topaz,' he blurted out. 'Whoever told you I was married?'

She felt a mixture of embarrassment, relief, joy, and stupidity. 'Róisín said you stayed in New York because of a woman. That's why you didn't return to Ireland,' Topaz said, feeling somewhat flustered.

'That was more than twenty five years ago!' he said, not hiding his exasperation. 'Do you really think I'd plead with you to come to dinner or come and stay at my home when it's so darn clear what I think of you, if I was *married*?' Now he felt somewhat embarrassed for exposing how vulnerable he felt about her. 'You do feel it too, don't you? When we met outside the café, you felt it, surely?' he asked hesitantly. 'Not all men are bastards, Topaz. You need to understand that.'

'Yes. I felt it, Connor. I haven't stopped feeling "it", whatever "it" is,' she sighed. 'What do you mean not all men are bastards?' Topaz asked.

'Never mind. Coffee or tea?'

'Coffee, thanks. What do you mean not all men are bastards? I never said you were one,' she blurted out, feeling that she'd wrongly accused him.

'If a bad mechanic messes with your car, you don't blame future mechanics and hold it against them. I feel you've kept me at arm's length because of...'

'A mechanic? What are you talking about?'

'Whatever has happened to you in the past with a man doesn't have to affect *us*. Can't we get to know each other without the memory of some bad boy standing between you and I?' he asked, his voice softening again.

'Connor, what do you know about my past relationships?' she asked, indignantly.

'Relationship,' he said, correcting her, with a slight smile on his lips.

'Is there anything you don't know about me, Connor Murphy?'

'Far too much. And I want to change that...' And there was that smile again.

He looked at her thoughtfully. 'If the human heart can survive the betrayal of someone they love and trust, it can survive anything.'

Connor led her into the lounge, and they sat side by side on the sofa.

'Haven't you been hurt in love before, Connor?' she dared to ask.

'Of course I have. It's part of life. You can't hope to go through life without having your heart broken at least once.'

'So who was she? What did she do to you?'

'So long ago I can't remember,' he pretended.

'What I do know is that I'm not into fast-food relationships via speed dating or Internet chat rooms. I'm an old fashioned boy, and I've always trusted that my soulmate was walking this Earth and that our paths would cross,' he smiled. 'Let's head downstairs shortly, and I can show you the bookshop and introduce you to some of the staff? The launch is at 4pm tomorrow afternoon. By the way, the cover illustration blew me away. I thought the black-and-white sketches were incredible, but wow...' he smiled. 'It was like you were right inside my head.'

'No, you were inside mine,' she insisted. Topaz felt an unfamiliar part of her body start to pulse with excitement. She'd felt dead in that area for way too long. Now her mind started to race. Would they end up sleeping together? Her breathing quickened. She wasn't ready for that. This was all happening way too quickly.

'Really?' he laughed, and grabbed her by the hand. 'Come on,' he said excitedly, almost like a young boy about to show off his train set.

'This is Barbara, my shop manager. My right-hand girl,' he said, introducing a rather tall, striking, Malibu-blonde woman in her late thirties. 'I couldn't run this place without her!'

'Pleased to meet you,' she purred.

Topaz smiled meekly. She wasn't sure if she should be pleased there was such a competent woman at his side. Was that jealousy stirring its ugly head in the pit of her stomach? *Oh go away!* she hissed to the voice in her head.

Topaz took great delight in following Connor around the shop. Although it was the largest bookstore she'd ever been in, there was something incredibly cosy about it. Every section was like a room in itself, bedecked with cushions, pot plants, billowy fabric hanging from the ceiling, child-sized chairs and beds for reading comfort. There were areas for colouring in, and listening to CDs. On the speaker was a Putumayo Children's CD *Jazz Playground*.

In the centre of the shop, on the first floor, was a child-sized walking labyrinth made of mosaic tiles. Young children were walking around it. Every part of the shop had a theme in the various spaces created: Jungle Room, Black Beauty, Cinderella, Harry Potter, etc. It was truly a child's fantasy land.

It was impossible not to feel good in here, and then she wondered if that's why Connor looked like he spent his whole life smiling ~ because he worked in a place that was so pleasant, joyful and was bringing love to the world. And then she felt her heart change direction. This gorgeous man beside her, with chiselled features, and an infectious smile, had grown up in the shadow of a deceased sibling. Was this shop his way of somehow healing an old wound? Her thoughts turned to *Mosaic*... Suddenly so much of it seemed like *his* autobiography rather than hers. He had to enter the Underworld and experience the dark; to walk Persephone's path before coming back to the light again. But then again, wasn't it every person's story?

She was disturbed from her thoughts by Barbara calling over. 'Connor, there's a phone call for you. Can you take it?'

'Excuse me,' he apologised to Topaz.

She made herself comfortable in a den made of tree trunks and sea-grass matting. No wonder children loved it here. It was a safe haven, and beautiful. All of the senses were nourished, and gave a person a feeling of comfort.

132

'Ah, I found you,' he smiled warmly, a few minutes later, crawling under the canopy made from twigs.

'This is amazing. Really amazing. You must be so proud of this place. It's such a work of art. You've added so many other things since the last time I visited here a few years ago,' she said.

'Thank you for noticing. It's been a lifetime's work,' he admitted.

'How will things change for you after the book's released tomorrow? I mean, will you write more books? How will you fit in the demands of being a popular author with this full-time job?' she asked, also aware of the growing feelings she had for him and the absurdity of falling for a man who lived thousands of miles away.

'It's all part of my life's plan,' he smiled mischievously.

'Your mum should be here,' she said sadly, looking down at the floor. 'She loves you so much. Why didn't you tell her about this book?'

'Never mind my mother! I know she loves me. It might surprise you to know that the feeling's mutual,' he grinned. 'She'll see the book soon enough. Now, we've got a big day tomorrow. I think we should get some rest. You know how exhausting all that meeting and greeting the adoring public is,' he chuckled. 'Everything here is organised. Barbara's got it all under control. How about I take you out for dinner?'

'How about I cook you dinner?' she said.

'Now there's an offer I can't refuse. Let's go!'

They climbed out of the den and headed back upstairs to Connor's apartment.

'You really do have a beautiful touch with décor, Connor. That's unusual in a man,' she said.

'I'm an unusual man,' he replied.

'Yes, I'm noticing that!' They laughed together gently.

Topaz rummaged through the fridge and pulled out a couple of punnets of mushrooms. 'My favourite vegetable!' she said.

'Snap. Mine too.' And their eyes lingered long enough to make the mushrooms blush.

Roughly chopping some garlic and tomatoes, Topaz then placed them in a casserole dish with the mushrooms. Drizzling glugs of olive oil around the dish, she then sprinkled sea salt and dried rosemary. 'They need about 30 minutes,' Topaz said; and then she could feel Connor's strong arms wrap around her waist.

Breath caught in her throat. There was that feeling again. This was where she belonged. 'Do you believe in love at first sight, Topaz?' he asked softly, with a sincerity that touched her right to the core of her being.

'I suppose anything's possible,' she replied. Topaz turned around to face him. 'It doesn't matter what I feel for you. I don't want a long-distance relationship. I'm not cut out for that sort of way of life.'

'Who is suggesting that?' he asked tenderly.

She suddenly felt foolish. Maybe he just wanted sex after all and she'd misread all the signals thinking it was more.

'I fell in love with you many years ago,' he said, staring right into her eyes. I saw your artwork in *Papa Possum's Day Off,* and I realise this sounds stupid, I knew I had to meet you. There was something about your artwork that was different to everyone else's. You weren't going to compromise. You stayed true to you and to children, offering them illustrations that were honest, beautiful, reflective and creative. I know it sounds ridiculous, but when I flicked to the back of the book and saw your artist's photo, I ... I just couldn't stop looking into your eyes. I knew then and there that one day we'd be together, no matter what. I can't explain how I knew.'

'Wasn't that a bit presumptuous?' Topaz asked. 'I mean, I could have been married. I could have been a lesbian. I could have…'

'Yes, you could have been a lot of things,' he said, putting his finger to her lips. 'But you weren't. And then, a short time later, I met Jack and Jess when they were holidaying in New York. I told them about this amazing artist, and well, you can imagine how I felt when they said that you were a friend of the family! And that you lived in the same part of the county as my mother. Suddenly the world seemed a whole lot smaller, and possible. One day my mum told me she'd met this lovely children's illustrator and I knew, I just *knew*, it was you. I couldn't believe you were so close to being in my life. It was just a matter of time.'

'Have I been set up?' Topaz laughed, hands on hips in mock protest. 'Is there such a thing as free will?'

'Yes, there is. You're free to walk out this door,' he said, hoping that she wouldn't, and embracing her just a little bit tighter.

'And who'd cook the mushrooms?' she asked in a serious tone. 'Ever since we met at the café, I haven't been able to get you out of my mind. And then when Jack introduced us, things started to make sense to me. Mosaic felt so personal when I read it. It was like you'd written it for me. You did, didn't you? Jack told you about Andy, didn't he?' Topaz asked.

'Yes. Yes, he did. And I wasn't going to let some

young guy, who didn't know how lucky he was, get in the way of us being together!' he insisted.

'But how could you even know that I'd feel like this for you?' Topaz asked.

'I followed my heart. Of course I had no way of knowing, not in a logical sense, but deep inside I just felt that everything in my life was drawing me to you, or maybe it was drawing you to me.' His hand touched her cheek. 'And then one day, there you were standing in The Labyrinth, browsing. I nearly fell out of my chair. You were there for two hours, and I didn't get an inch of work done. My eyes followed you everywhere, just taking you in. I was captivated. Mesmerised. Enchanted. Then, I knew it was just a matter of time until we'd meet properly.'

'Just a matter of time...' she repeated after him. 'But why didn't you come and say hello? Why didn't you introduce yourself then?'

'Tongue-tied, I guess. I was in awe of you,' he admitted.

Connor leant down and brushed his cheek softly against her skin, his eyes closing while he let his sense of touch take her in. Slowly lifting his hands to the back of her head, he kissed her as gently as if he were touching a newborn baby. Their kisses were slow and tender, and Topaz thought her legs would collapse beneath her as both knees went weak. Blood was pulsing through every part of her body, and she could feel that this was happening to him too. It felt so good to feel that he was attracted to her; that Connor Murphy wanted her not just in his imagination but in every part of his manly body. *He wanted her.*

They eventually pulled away and lovingly looked into each other's eyes.

'I found you,' he whispered as tears fell down

her cheeks. 'It's okay, you can cry,' and he ever-so-gently wiped her free-falling salty tears.

'Your mother tells me the same thing,' she laughed through her crying.

The oven buzzer made them both jump. Topaz said, 'I'll just make the rest,' reluctantly removing herself from his embrace.

Quickly, she made a tomato sauce by sautéeing some onions, garlic, and dried herbs. She added a few handsome spoons of tomato paste, a bit of water, a slosh of red wine, a drizzle of balsamic vinegar and a little maple syrup. Connor dipped his finger into the sauce. 'Mmmm, that's good!' And then he made the fatal mistake of grabbing a spoon so he could keep eating.

'Get out of there! And don't tell anyone the secret recipe,' she ordered, shaking the wooden spoon at him.

Breadcrumbs sautéed alongside flaked almonds, in a little olive oil; then Topaz added some seasoning. Carefully pouring the tomato sauce over the roast mushrooms, she sprinkled the breadcrumb mixture on top, and placed it in the oven for another ten minutes, until it was golden on top.

Connor was instructed to make a salad.

'For a bachelor, you sure have a lot of food in the house,' she smirked.

'Even bachelors need to keep up their energy!' he argued.

'Especially when they have lady visitors come to stay?'

'Yes, indeed.'

Connor set the table, and lit a candle. Turning the CD player on, Topaz was touched to hear the first movement of a Mozart sonata.

'You like Mozart?'

He looked at her quizzically. 'Something wrong with Mozart?'

'No, just wondered if you read that on one of my artist biographies somewhere,' she said suspiciously.

'Not at all. I played Mozart a lot during my schoolboy piano lessons. He grew on me pretty quickly.'

They enjoyed a peaceful dinner, their feet touching underneath the table, comforting, caressing and teasing each other. 'This is so much nicer than going out to dinner. Thank you for suggesting it,' he said.

'I much prefer eating at home. I like to see what goes into my food,' Topaz said thoughtfully. 'Yeah, I know, you're going to tell me I have "trust" issues,' she laughed.

'Wouldn't dream of it,' he said, raising a glass. 'Here's to us.'

'Us,' she echoed.

After dinner, he washed and she dried. Topaz had never enjoyed doing the dishes so much in her life. There was something about this scene of domesticity that felt comfortable and reassuring. *Is this what organic love is like?*, she wondered. *It just happens so easily.* She thought about a conversation she once had with her *Does Life Begin at Forty?* friends. 'How do you know when you've met the right person?' Topaz had asked them. Róisín had replied without hesitation, 'Because you don't have to ask, you just know.'

They retired to the open-plan lounge, relaxing in each other's arms and talking about their lives. After a while, Topaz asked, 'Where are your cats?'

'What cats?' he replied, somewhat bemused by the question.

'Italics and Grammar' she said.

Connor laughed out loud. 'I don't have cats.'

'But...on your author biography you said you live with two cats! You mean you lied to your readers?'

'No, I didn't lie. I do have two cats. Come and see.' He pulled her by the hand to his writing room. 'There!' On the window sill were two porcelain black cats that served as book ends. 'Italics and Grammar.'

'I might have fallen in love with you based on those two cats!' she grinned.

'Well *that* would be silly, wouldn't it?' he chided.

'Yes, almost as silly as falling in love with someone from their artwork or their photo!' But she couldn't protest, as his lips were on hers, soothing away any thoughts she had of fraud.

'Fallen in love, you say?' he smiled.

'Might have, I said,' but she knew that it was out in the open. No more pretending. No more hiding.

'I'd love two cats. We had a dozen or so when I was a child. Mum was always bringing home a stray,' he reminisced.

'I can just imagine her doing that!' Topaz giggled. 'She still does, come to think of it!'

'I miss having real cats around, and one day when I'm living on land again I'll have a couple,' he confided, his arms tightly around her waist.

'You mean you can see a day when you don't own The Labyrinth?' she asked. 'But it's your whole life,' Topaz added, defending the business that he'd built from the ground up.

'It's part of my life, and I've loved every day of it, but it's not my whole life. I grew up in the country. I've always been a country boy at heart. I wasn't born to wear a suit and tie!' he said.

He looked at his watch. 'We should get some

sleep. It's a big day tomorrow. Jack and Jess are arriving first thing in the morning, and I'm expecting the delivery of books at noon.'

'Are you sure you're happy with the black and white artwork?' she asked with a hint of nervousness.

'You know I love it!' he reassured her.

'And the cover,' she said confidently, 'I've made sure your readers can judge *Mosaic* by its cover,' Topaz smiled. 'Goodnight, then,' she said and slipped away to her room.

'Hey, come back here,' and he gently grabbed her hand and kissed her softly on the cheek. 'Sleep well.'

Topaz showered, and enjoyed the jasmine soap that was sitting by the towel rail. *That's why he smells so good*, she thought, realising the scent made her think she was in her very own garden. No wonder she felt at home in his arms!

Drying herself with a thick, large, aubergine-coloured towel made from Egyptian cotton, Topaz looked at herself in the mirror. It had been such a long day, and yet she saw colour in her cheeks and happiness in her eyes. She crawled into bed and realised that sleep was going to evade her despite her tiredness. All Topaz could think about was Connor lying in the next room. Oh how she'd enjoyed his arms around her. And where did he learn to kiss like that? Clearly he hadn't lived as a monk. She glanced at the clock: 12.30am. *Get some sleep girl*, she told herself furiously.

Topaz thought she'd heard a gentle knock on her door. 'May I come in?' Connor whispered.

'Yes,' she said, her heart pounding.

'I can't sleep. Mind if I lie beside you?' he asked.

She lifted up the blanket for him to get in beside her.

Connor wrapped his arms around her, and whispered 'Goodnight'. Within minutes they were both sound asleep. They awoke at first light, and lay looking into each other's eyes for some time without talking.

'Why didn't you make love to me last night?' Topaz asked boldly. 'Is there something wrong with me?' She surprised herself by the questions coming out of her mouth.

'A relationship is only as good as the friendship it is based on. I want to make love to you more than you could ever imagine, but I want you to know that I'm a swan.'

Topaz looked at him curiously. 'A swan? What are you talking about?'

He looked at her with sincerity. 'A swan mates for life. I'm not going anywhere Topaz. I've waited a very long time for you. I can wine and dine you, I can take you on hot dates. I can buy you perfume and clothes. But I want you to know that all those things are meaningless unless we actually enjoy each other's company.'

'You mean like when we were washing the dishes last night?' she asked.

'Yes, just like that. Day-to-day life can be quite mundane. What makes it amazing is the way we live it, and the way we go from morning to night each day. A wonderful life is based on lots of very ordinary moments. And besides, I'm going to make love to you for the rest of my life,' he smiled. 'In case you hadn't noticed, I've been making love with you from the moment I met you at the airport.'

She blushed, and then blushed some more as she

recalled how he truly had wooed her with his touch, love, laughter and kind gestures.

Connor pulled her closer. She could feel that he did indeed want to make love to her. There was that pulsing feeling again. *How could he be so controlled?*, she wondered, when all she wanted to do was rip her pyjamas off and feel him inside her, around her, consuming her. For him to enter that secret, sacred cavern of pleasure reserved for him, and him alone.

'Jack and Jess are bringing a surprise. We'd best get up and get on with the day,' he sighed, knowing that neither of them wanted to leave the bed.

'I'll just have a shower and get us some breakfast. Would you like a smoothie, fruit salad, toast?' he asked.

'Nothing. I'm not hungry. Maybe a juice?' she said.

Topaz showered, and washed her hair. She took some time getting dressed, and wore an ankle-length, forest-green, fitted, long velvet skirt with zigzagged satin ribbons at the back, and a matching crocheted cardigan over a cream-coloured blouse. As she stepped into the kitchen, she smiled to see Connor in a cream, long-sleeved muslin shirt and tight, dark-blue denim jeans. He hadn't shaved for quite a few days, and she found his stubble rather becoming as it ignited a primal urge deep within her.

Connor was humming. She was surprised that he wasn't wearing a business suit, but clearly he was defining his image as an author rather than as a businessman.

'Here,' he said, passing her a freshly squeezed orange juice.

'Mmmm, thank you,' she said, letting her hands touch his on the glass.

142

Topaz sat down at the dining table. Connor was tidying up the chopping board, knife and juicer, and starting his tune again, this time, singing:

If tomorrow never comes
Will she know how much I loved her
Did I try in every way, to show her every day
That she's my only one

She recognised the Garth Brooks country ballad.
'That's a sad song,' she said.
'Is it?' he asked.
'Well yes! The lyrics go on to say:

If my time on Earth were through
And she must face this world without me
Is the love I gave her in the past, gonna be enough to last.

'Is it really sad to be loved so much by someone that their love carries you through life even if they're no longer at your side?' he asked in a way that was so touching it brought tears to her eyes: Almost as if he understood what it was to love, and then lose. And then Topaz remembered Connor's dad's death, and Róisín having to pull up her socks and live life without him. How his death ~ how his *love* ~ had given her the courage to let go of their life in Ireland and start anew in the north of England.

'If the love was that great she wouldn't want to go on without him!' she said emphatically.

He smiled. 'Are you ready to go down to the shop? Come on, I want you to see the surprise.'

'Is Jack's surprise for me?' she asked.

'It's for both of us!' His cheeky grin made her curious. Sometimes he was just like a boy such was his

143

enthusiasm for life. *His joy is contagious*, she thought to herself.

'What is it?' she asked.

'Come and see for yourself!' And together, hand in hand, they went to The Labyrinth. It was already busy with people, many of them arriving early for the book launch. Quite a lot had been customers of the shop for years, and some of the younger parents remembered growing up here and spending hours in one of the dens, reading. The publicity that Connor Murphy, owner of the legendary Children's Labyrinth, had written a children's novel meant that all the city's journalists were camped out on the pavement.

'I'm feeling claustrophobic,' she confided to Connor, holding his hand tightly. He stopped, and looked her right in the eyes. She noticed how the colour of his eyes matched the clothes she was wearing. 'Just breathe deeply. Imagine your feet have roots going down deep into the earth. Breathe slowly and deeply. You're safe,' he promised her. 'Let me tell you again how much I love the colour cover illustration. It's perfect.'

And just then she saw the exhibition posters and banners featuring *Mosaic*. The store had metamorphosed over night. 'Barbara must have been up all night!' Topaz said, empathising with the lack of sleep.

'And her team of helpers!' he said, looking over the tables filled with finger foods and drinks.

'There's Jack!' Connor said excitedly, pointing through the crowds.

But it wasn't Jack that Topaz saw first. It was Róisín! Topaz cried tears of joy. She'd grown to love Róisín dearly, and felt it highly unfair that Connor hadn't told her about the book. But here she was, right here, right now, in this bookshop for the launch.

'When did you tell your mum?' she asked, wondering if this was another fib right up there with the porcelain cats.

'I didn't. Jack did, and made sure she had a plane fare booked. Do you really think I wouldn't tell her? I just wanted to make sure all my plans were in place,' he said, rushing faster through the crowd while securely holding her hand.

'Mum!' he exclaimed, lifting her into the air like she was a toddler!

'Put me down,' she giggled. 'Connor Murphy, put me down!' They hugged for the longest time.

'My darling girl,' Róisín said when she embraced Topaz. 'What are these tears for? Joy, I hope.'

'Joy,' she sniffed, nodding her head affirmatively. 'Joy.'

Jack and Jess came forward and hugged her and Connor.

'Shall we go into my office for a bit of breathing room?' Connor suggested, and led the way.

Topaz admired the way he looked so comfortable in this world even though he said he was a country boy. She thought about her own life, in rural England, and wondered if their lives really would be joined in some way. Or did he expect her to give up her life and move to America. The thought shocked her. *How could she leave Saph? How could she leave Cumbria?*

There was a coffee machine in his office, and Connor started taking orders for a latte, cappuccinos and espresso. Coffee and bookshops seemed to be made for each other, and Topaz marvelled at the difference between this bookshop and Sam's

Bookshop and Café in her Cumbrian market town. She felt an uncomfortable ache. Would Connor really ask her to leave England and move to the USA?

'How are you feeling, Connor?' Jack asked. 'Five publishers fought at auction for this book. That's quite an achievement.'

'Feeling good, actually. Ready for the next chapter in my life,' and he laughed at the writer's pun. 'The sale has gone through for The Labyrinth. The new owner takes over in January. As much as I love this place, it feels like a huge burden off my shoulders.'

'You've sold *The Labyrinth*!' Róisín said, startled at the revelation.

'Sold it?' Topaz repeated after her, feeling a little dizzy.

'Why?' Róisín asked. 'This is your everything.'

'It's my something, Mum, not my everything.' And he reached for Topaz's hand.

'What are you going to do?' his mother asked.

'Write books!' he laughed. 'That's my intention anyway. To return to the countryside and write books.'

'Ireland? You're going home to Ireland?' She seemed puzzled.

'No Mum, not Ireland. Home is where family is.' And he silently squeezed Topaz a bit tighter. I'm moving to Cumbria.'

Róisín gasped! 'Did you know about this Jack?'

'Yes, I did. I'm sorry for keeping the secret. Connor made me!' Jack said, in mock defence; and he backed away, laughing, in case she got angry with him.

'I forgive you!' And she hugged Connor tightly.

'Does this mean you might take Topaz on a date?' she asked cheekily.

'We've been on a date, Mum,' he winked.

Kissing by the Mistletoe

Jack called for everyone's attention over the sound system, and within a few seconds the shop became quiet. 'My name's Jack Ryland. I'm the owner of Ryland's Publishers, and it's my delight today to welcome you here to The Children's Labyrinth. I know many of you adults have been coming here for two and a half decades. It's such an honour for me to publish Connor Murphy's first novel, and I sincerely hope we can publish many more.'

There was loud applause throughout the shop. 'For those of you unfamiliar with Connor, please allow me to introduce you. Ladies, gentlemen and children: Connor Murphy.'

Connor walked up onto the makeshift stage to the sound of applause and cheers.

Connor looked so handsome; Topaz couldn't keep her eyes off him. The week-old stubble had an effect on her libido that was unshakeable. 'You're in love, aren't you?' Róisín whispered into her ear, smiling broadly.

'Is it that obvious?' Topaz asked.

'The pair of you look like you're made for each other.' And she put her arm around Topaz's waist. 'I couldn't be happier!'

'When we first met I asked you how you know if someone's the right person for you, and you said "because you don't have to ask"… Roisin, I haven't asked if Connor's the right one for me. I felt it the day we met outside Sam's. I knew that I'd remember his face, his smile, his eyes and his voice for the rest of my life, even if I never saw him again.'

Their eyes moistened at this open declaration.

Connor talked about the inspiration behind the book, and what it was like writing his first novel after years of promoting other people's books.

'But this book wouldn't be complete without the fine artwork of a beautiful lady, and talented artist. Topaz Lane has captured my imagination and my heart. I'm delighted to welcome her here today. Topaz, would you please come up here and join me for the unveiling of our book?' he asked with that irresistible cheeky-boy grin that beckoned her every time.

She tilted her head to one side and gave him a mock glare. 'Topaz?' he asked, in a tone that she couldn't refuse.

Topaz could feel Róisín push against her back. 'Go.'

As she joined him on stage, Topaz was acutely aware of the photographers' flash cameras on overdrive. Connor reached over and kissed her on the lips. *Such a public display of affection*, she thought.

'On the count of three?' he teased; and together they opened the velvet curtains concealing thousands of books.

'May we present *Mosaic*! If you'd like a signed copy, Topaz and I will be here for the afternoon and are more than happy to oblige. There's plenty of great food and drinks. Please help yourself.'

There was loud applause, and shop staff brought boxes of books to the counter. They sold like hotcakes.

Topaz and Connor seated themselves at a long table to begin the signing process. She pulled a gold, engraved fountain pen, that her father had once given her, out of her bag, and smiled at the first person in the queue. 'Hi, thank you so much for coming today. Who would you like this signed to?' she asked, after the person had had their copy signed by Connor.

'For Stephanie,' the young teenage girl smiled.

Topaz opened the book to sign, but it fell a few pages in rather than at the title page. And there she saw words that weren't on the manuscript that Jacqueline had sent through to her. It read:

For Topaz,
my happily ever after.

She could hardly hold back the tears. Even then, he'd been so confident; so sure that she would say yes. Topaz signed the book, and then looked over to Connor who was busy cracking jokes. How could such a funny boy be so confident, and committed to her?

'Can you sign it for Jessica, please?' came the voice of the next person in the line.

'Of course,' Topaz smiled. *My happily ever after;* she kept playing the words through her head over and over again.

It was several hours before the queue died down. Róisín had kept them topped up with drinks. When the doors closed at 9pm, Topaz said to Connor, 'Would you like me to sign your copy?'

'If I can sign yours,' he said.

'I think you already have,' she smiled. Alongside the decorations, crooners sang out Christmas songs over the sound system.

He passed her a copy of their book. She turned to the dedication page, and wrote: *For my swan. Thank you for waiting for me. Thank you for understanding. May I always be a good-enough swan for you, because, if tomorrow never comes...I will know how much you loved me.*

Connor choked up as he read the words, and

thought about the song. 'Come with me,' he said, and led her to the mistletoe decoration nearby as the song, *Kissing by the Mistletoe*, played on the sound system.

With tenderness, he caressed her lower back, and brought their bodies together. She kissed him first, her lips tingling as they met.

'Are you really moving to Cumbria?' she asked hesitantly.

'I will move to the ends of the Earth to be near you, and I hope that wherever that place is, my mother will be there, too.'

She sighed deeply as his soft stubble pressed gently into her cheek. 'I'm glad you found me, because I've been looking for you for a long time.' Their moment of passion was interrupted.

'Hey Connor, Jess and I are going to call it a night. We'll come by tomorrow before we fly back home. What a fantastic launch that was,' Jack said, reaching out to shake Connor's hand. 'There are only twenty books left out of two thousand. I've made sure there's another delivery tomorrow. Jacqueline texted me to say there've been sell-outs in London, too.'

'Mum, you're coming back to my place aren't you?' Connor asked, but had already presumed.

'Of course. I'm flying back tomorrow with Jack and Jess. I want to have every second with you that I can.'

They headed upstairs, and had a nightcap in Connor's apartment. 'I'll make a bed up for you Mum. I'll just be a minute.'

He changed the sheets on his bed, and showed her into the room. 'I know you have the guest room when you're here, but I hope you won't mind sleeping in my room tonight?' he winked, thinking of Topaz, who now had the guest room.

'Not at all,' she winked back. 'Good night you two, and well done. That was such a fantastic day. I'm so proud of you both.'

'Goodnight Róisín,' Topaz said, hugging her warmly.

'Coming to bed honey?' Connor asked Topaz.

Honey, she thought. That sounds so nice. *Yes, I'm his honey.*

'I know your return flight is tomorrow, but could you stay at least one more night? Please?' His voice came softly from between the curve of her breasts, where his cheek was resting

She could feel the ache inside his body. One more night? Of course she could. They fell asleep in each other's arms, content that this was the beginning of their life together.

They left the bookshop at noon, and headed out into the snow to the waiting cab. There was a tearful goodbye with Róisín, Jack and Jess.

'I'll call you when I get home,' Topaz promised Róisín. 'As soon as the plane lands,' she said.

'Barbara, I'm going to be unavailable for the rest of the day. Can you handle things?' Connor asked.

'Yes, no problem,' she said, and Topaz couldn't believe that Connor had never hooked up with her. Beauty on his doorstep. How could he refuse that?

Once they were back in his apartment, Topaz shared what was on her mind.

'Barbara is beautiful…' she said, hoping he'd follow her lead.

'Yes, she is. Beautiful, intelligent, witty, sophisticated, with an encyclopaedic knowledge of

151

children's literature. And you're wondering if I've ever slept with her, aren't you? The answer is no, not even close. Not remotely tempted. There's no need to be jealous. There's no chemistry with her. Not from my side, anyway.'

'I don't understand that you're 45 years old and not in a relationship. How's that even possible?'

He frowned and pulled her close. 'I thought I *was* in a relationship,' he said, with an unfamiliar sadness in his eyes.

'I meant married.'

'I intend to be,' he smiled. 'Will you marry me, Topaz Lane?' Connor asked, bending down on one knee.

Laughing out loud, she said, 'I wasn't trying to get a proposal!' and she tried to pull him up off his bended knee.

Topaz followed him to her bedroom. He lit a candle, and pulled the curtains closed. Connor undressed her, and whispered, 'Time for some afternoon delight. May I make love to you now?'

'I never thought you'd ask!' she giggled, a little nervously.

The busy world outside the window came to a standstill. The heat of their bodies led them further towards each other. Connor brushed his cheek against her breasts and sighed as he placed his head between them. They enjoyed feeling each other's skin; their hands touching and caressing every part of each other's body. Some time later, Connor felt the dampness between her legs and knew she was ready. With deliberate gentleness, he entered her without apology. This was what they both wanted. This was not the rushed sex of movies, or indeed her experience with Andy, engineered with empty grunts and banging. No, this was different: slow, kind and thoughtful lovemaking.

Like a perfectly fitting key, he opened the door to another world. Her whole body received him, and he felt her open up more and more; inviting him in further and deeper. The artist in Topaz couldn't help but feel that it was as if he were using a paintbrush to magnificently paint the ceiling of her dark cathedral. Each brush stroke, conscious and intentional, purposefully bringing the masterpiece closer to completion, until they reached the sacred shrine of their devotion.

They marvelled at how the differences between a man and a woman could be so compatible. Their affectionate lovemaking was a seamless blend of selfishness and annihilation of the ego as they surrendered and became one. This is what he'd waited years for, and this ~ *this* ~ is why Topaz had closed her heart. She instinctively knew that nothing less than this was good enough for her. She just hadn't recognised it till now.

'I love you Connor,' her voice came out breathlessly between moans of ecstasy.

'I thought I'd grow on you,' he laughed. 'You're so beautiful,' Connor whispered; and together they climbed the great mountain of ecstasy, waves of pleasure rippling through their bodies like waves repeatedly lapping upon the shoreline until, eventually, they were satiated. The beauty and brilliance of orgasm, in all its irony: a death of sorts; a surrendering, a letting go. Sometime later, they fell asleep in each other's arms.

One day, Connor Murphy would tell her how turned on he was by her complete abandon, and how her moans of pleasure rivalled the NY Fire-

153

Department sirens on a busy day. But for now, he smiled and thought how darn lucky he was to be with such a responsive woman.

'I'll be in England as soon as I can. I need to be here for the handover in January, and for the paperwork to be finalised,' he said, feeling the sadness creeping between both of them when he escorted her to the airport.

'But that's weeks away, Connor,' complained Topaz.

'I know,' he said, kissing her forehead. 'But it will fly by, I promise. I'll phone you every night. I'll email. I'll skype.'

'NO SKYPING!' she laughed.

Topaz didn't hide the tears, which flowed freely. And nor did Connor. 'We're over the worst bit. We're together now. The ocean is just an illusion. We're together in our hearts. I promise we'll be together soon.' He kissed her one last time. 'I love you Topaz Lane.'

They reluctantly let each other go as the last boarding call was made.

The Dark Womb

Connor, in utero

This place is dark and heavy. The light rarely shines. I hear her cry all the time. I want to get out. And yet, she writes me letters. Kind and beautiful words telling me how very much she wants me in her life, and that she loves me. My mother apologises that her heart is still so heavy. She reads these letters aloud to me, and my father, in bed each night by candlelight. In her journal, she invites me here into her world saying how much she's looking forward to meeting me.

Mother shares her deepest fears with me, too. She doesn't feel she'll ever get through the grief from when my sister, Eden, was taken so cruelly from her world. She ebbs and flows in this journal. There are moments when she's high and bright and telling me about the baby clothes she's sewing me, and then there are days when she says she left a shop, running, because the tears came up so unexpectantly.

Mother writes that her life feels like treacle. Every step is slow and painful. She feels no freedom. Mother acknowledges that she wanted to conceive me so very desperately, and hoped that I'd take away the pain of losing Eden. I haven't, she discovered. She's sad. So am I. I can never replace my sister.

We touch hands, Eden and I. You see, I'm not fully of this world yet. I'm still aware of where I came from before being conceived, and here I play with Eden.

I can see her love for Mother, but both of us know that Mother isn't aware of it. It doesn't stop us trying to make her smile, though. I hope that my gentle kicks against her belly will make her laugh; that they'll remind her that I'm here: alive, and in her womb. I'm here, getting ready to come into the world...

It's time now. As I make my way down the dark tunnel, I see the light of Eden slipping away from me, and I'm soon blinded by another light. It's excruciating. Hands grab me. I scream for just a moment from the shock of gravity. I'm here. *I'm here!*

I'm born on this snowy Winter's night by a blazing open fire.

My father takes me in his hands and passes me to my mother. I feel her love. Their love. They have poor pockets but their hearts are rich. I have chosen the right parents for me.

Monet and Matisse

'Hello, Barbara speaking,' purred the voice at the end of Connor's phone.

Topaz couldn't speak. What was *she* doing there! In his apartment! On a Sunday!

'Hello?' Barbara repeated to the silence at the end of the line.

'Er, it's Topaz. Is Connor there?' she asked, feeling as if she was invading their space. *Don't be ridiculous*, she kept telling herself. *She works for him, they're not lovers!*

'No, he's not. Sorry, you, er, just missed him.'

'Okay, thanks.' She had barely hung up the phone before dissolving into a puddle of tears. They'd phoned every day, sometimes twice a day, since Topaz returned to England. Every phone call was deep and honest. They'd talked about their joys, confided their fears, and discussed how they wanted to raise their children in a respectful, compassionate way. She reflected on how she felt reading *The Continuum Concept*, and about Camira's birth. It wasn't a surprise that Connor felt passionately about having a home birth, given his mother's passion for natural birth. Topaz shared how much she'd learnt about mothering from Camira. She knew that Connor and her were reading off the same page. Their children, *their* children, would be raised in a gentle way, together.

So why was *she* in his apartment? Topaz went to bed early. Just her and a hot-water bottle and the radio.

'This evening we're featuring the brilliant Irish singer-songwriter, Mandy Bingham, who was recently on tour here in Cumbria. *Matter of Time,'* came the radio announcer's deep voice through Topaz's bedroom, 'is my favourite song of hers. I hope you enjoy it as much as I do.'

Only a matter of time till you're not mine…
Why do you stay when you're so already gone?
Why make me pay
I don't know what I did wrong.

Only a matter of time till you're not mine…

It was only a matter of time until her pillow was soaked in salt water. She got up and had a hot shower. Standing there, for the longest time, she let the comforting warm water wash away her pain. Steam filled the bathroom, creating an illusion of warmth on such a bitterly cold and icy Winter's night.

How could this have happened to her again? She thought Connor was different. He *promised* that he wasn't Andy, or like other men, and she, stupidly, believed him.

Dressing in flannel pyjamas, she went and phoned Sapphire. Sobbing down the phone, she finally got the words out.

'Topaz, he loves you. I'm sure there's an explanation. Connor isn't like that. You've got to trust him,' Sapphire insisted, but not convincingly enough to ease Topaz's aching heart. She crawled back into bed and cried. The bed she was meant to share with her swan. Where was he?

Good Girl Blues by Mandy Bingham was the soundtrack she fell asleep to in the deep of the night.

Morning came early for Topaz, despite the Winter darkness. She rose before six, and lit the woodstove

158

and the Aga. Today she would bake. *Baking heals everything*, she reassured herself.

Today was Christmas Eve, the time she traditionally celebrated Christmas in the spirit of her European ancestry. She'd begged Sapphire and Jeff to spend this Christmas on their own as symbolic of the family unit they were creating. And now she was biting her tongue. Oh how she longed for their company. At the time, she'd been feeling brave and strong and more than willing to celebrate on her own, and to then share Christmas day with Róisín.

Róisín. *I'm not going to cry*, she told herself as she thought of her dear friend, and then realised the irony: Róisín would be the first person to tell her to cry.

The kitchen soon filled with the smell of Christmas: cloves, ginger, cinnamon, honey, maple syrup, almond essence. Topaz realised she was going a bit overboard with the number of spicy Christmas cookies she baked, but she consoled herself that it would bring a lot of good cheer to the people she delivered them to later in the day: Róisín, Francesca, Lia, Annie, Camira, Kate and Sapphire.

Radio Birch was on softly in the background, like an old friend. 'A bitterly cold day here in the valley,' came the familiar voice of Josh Landing. 'Stay rugged up! Cumbria is going to freeze over today. And now, this is the awesomely talented singer-songwriter, Lily Juniper, with her hit song, *Plan B*. Have a great day.'

Topaz put the kettle on, and washed up the last of the mixing bowls. *Plan B*, she mused with heavy heart. *Yes, I need a Plan B.*

A knock at the front door startled her. A pan of parsnip and apple soup was taken off the heat; Topaz removed her flour-dusted apron, and headed over. When she opened it, no-one was there. A cat carrier was on the doorstep with an envelope taped to the top. Inside the carrier was a beautiful ginger and white kitten, about seven months old, letting out small meows. Topaz looked around the garden and tilted her head to see down the road. Sapphire? she wondered. Opening the envelope quickly, she read: *'Dear Matisse, Everyone needs a friend. My name's Monet. Merry Christmas.'*

'Sorry puss,' she apologised to the cat, and stepped around the cat cage and ran gingerly down the snowy path; and she kept running when she got past the gate. *Who dropped this here?* Sapphire knew Topaz wanted a feline companion for her cat, but why would she leave it on the doorstep and not say hello? With no sign of who delivered it, Topaz slowed down and caught her breath. Feeling despondent that she had such a personal gift and didn't know who it was from or how it got here, she headed back to the house. She noticed fox tracks, and bird tracks, and the shoe prints she'd left in the snow, and the tracks the visitor had made to her house. And then, she realised that they only led to the house. They hadn't left.

Walking up the garden, she thought of the new kitten out in the cold, and looked up to find a tall man standing on the doorstep: waving and smiling that cheeky grin! *Connor!*

Without a thought, Topaz ran up the snowy garden path and straight into his arms. She was never going to part from him again, no matter what.

'I love you Connor. I love you.'

'I know. I know you love me, and you know how deeply I love you, right? It's time now. Time for us to be together. Let nothing get in the way of that. Now, shall we get this little fella some food and water?' he smiled.

160

'I'll move to New York if I have to, but I don't want to spend another day apart,' she insisted.

'You don't need to do that. I'm here to stay. If you'll have me, that is. And Italics and Grammar aren't far behind. If you'll have them too!' he laughed.

'Of course I'll have you!' Tears trickled down her cheeks. She felt foolish, but she had to tell him. 'I phoned last night but Barbara answered...' Topaz didn't need to utter another word. He knew what she was thinking.

'Oh sweetheart,' he said reassuringly. 'My sweetheart, I can't make you trust me, but I hope you'll learn to see that I'm just not wired that way. I know what it's like to have someone sleep with your best friend. I know what it's like to have your heart thrown away as if it's paper.'

She looked into his eyes with deep compassion. 'You do?'

'Yes...the woman I stayed in America for? Sometime I'll tell you, but let's get out of the cold. And what is that aroma? It's wonderful!' he said, carrying Monet into the warm cookie-filled kitchen.

'I thought you weren't coming till January,' she said, confused by his early arrival.

'That was the intention, but the paperwork went through quicker than we expected. And Barbara? Barbara was in my apartment for one reason only. She's the new owner of The Labyrinth. I was on a plane here when you phoned. The plane had been delayed because of weather conditions. I arrived in the early hours...far too early to knock on your door. I phoned Sapphire before I left, and arranged for her to pick me up from the train, and then we went to the animal rescue centre first thing.'

Topaz sobbed. 'Sapphire knew? No wonder she

was so calm last night,' she sighed. 'I'm so sorry for doubting you, for even a second. I didn't want to. It didn't feel right...'

'But old records were playing inside your head? I understand. The experiences of our lives are rather like sediment, aren't they? There's just layer upon layer of memory. If I've learnt anything, Topaz, it's this: don't ever make assumptions,' he said kindly, and then swept her up in his arms. She laughed with delight. 'Let's make both of us some new memories.'

Matisse, a three-year-old black cat, strolled into the kitchen and surveyed her new companion. She sniffed at the cat cage. *Company*, she thought.

'Got any cat litter?' Connor asked.

'So, straight into domestic life then?' Topaz asked, walking to the broom cupboard.

'What, you'd rather have wine and dinner in a restaurant than cats around your feet and Christmas cookies baking?' he laughed.

'No, never,' Topaz replied.

It Came Upon a Midnight Clear

Christmas Eve came in cheerily through the front door, gathering oranges, cloves and snowflakes on the way. Together Topaz and Connor prepared a celebratory meal for two. She ground up Brazil nuts, and fried them with onions and sunflower seeds to make a loaf layered with dried onion and sage stuffing. Slow-braised red cabbage with apple and nutmeg simmered on the stove top all afternoon. Connor peeled a few potatoes, and cut slivers into them to make saddleback potatoes. They roasted in the oven, alongside maple-glazed parsnips, and gingered honey carrots. At the last minute, he stir-fried sliced Brussels sprouts in garlic.

'Here's to the first of many Christmases that we will spend together,' Connor said, his Irish lilt warming their home. *Their* home. 'To those on our own, to those with friends, and to our Christmases with children at our feet.'

'To us,' Topaz smiled. 'This *is* real, isn't it?' she asked. 'Us?' and she sighed contentedly. 'Don't ever outgrow those laughing eyes of yours, Connor. I couldn't bear it.'

They ate far too much, and gathered by the woodstove after their meal. They played Christmas-carol duets on the piano, before letting a CD take over.

Topaz pulled off the paper around the gift from Connor. Inside she found a wall hanging. A finely needled tapestry of their home, with the words: *And they all lived happily ever after.*

She laughed, and said, 'How perfect. I love it. The question is, though, where do I hang it? Over our bed, or in the hallway so I can see it every time I step in the front door?'

'Hallway!' they both said in unison, recognising that family would soon be integral to their life.

'So, I guess this Christmas is about giving each other a message, then,' she smiled, passing Connor the gift she had for when he returned to England.

He opened it to find a fabric-bound journal with handmade paper she'd crafted, and little sketches, in the style of *Mosaic*, in the corners of some of the pages. On the cover were the Latin words: *Nulla dies sine linea*.

'Never a day without a line,' he said out loud.

'You remembered your Latin!' Topaz said in surprise. 'I thought I might have to translate. Don't ever stop writing, Connor. You have a real gift. Make sure you keep sharing it with the world.' And with that, she leant over to kiss him.

Paying It Forward

Over the next couple of months, Topaz embraced the dark Cumbrian Winter, and was thankful for the skylights Jeff had originally put into her artist studio so she could paint even on the gloomiest days. She was working on personal portraits, and devoted every waking day to getting them just right.

'Today's competition is…' and the familiar voice of Josh Landing invited callers to phone up. Topaz realised she'd not been in touch with the station to tell them about her birthday prize. She immediately phoned Radio Birch.

'Can you put me through to Josh Landing's private line, please? He'll remember me from the *Does Life Begin at 40?* competition.'

'Putting you through right now, Ms Lane.

'Josh speaking. Hello Ms Lane. I wondered if you'd ever get in touch.'

She laughed, and then said, 'I've been on quite a journey since then. I wondered if you might like to chat sometime, and maybe I could do an interview about it?'

They agreed to meet for lunch the next day. Josh invited her onto the programme, and together they talked about the women she met, and that life begins any time you give yourself permission. She shared how the women were each from a different decade, and yet their lives were so rich with meaning. As she left the studio, she knew it was time: Time for Topaz to give back to the women in her life.

She called each of the *Does Life Begin at 40?* women, and asked them to meet at her home that weekend. Connor was sent off to Saph and Jeff's place for the afternoon, and Saph and Camira were also called over.

As they gathered around her kitchen table drinking tea and coffee, and eating pear and nutmeg cake, she gave them each a copy of *Mosaic*. Kate laughed right out loud. 'Fabulous title!'

'You women have touched my life in ways I can't even begin to explain. You gave me gifts that came from your heart, and showed me who you are. You trusted me with your secrets, and with your pain. You spoke to me by what you said and by what you didn't say. You held my broken heart in your hands, and soothed it. I don't know if I can truly repay you, but I wanted to give you a copy of *Mosaic*. It's a personal story, and you all know about how Connor and I got together. I hope when you read it, though, that you'll be able to read your own stories, too. And that the book is the story of how you got through your own dark days. At first, all I could see was that each of you lived such charmed lives. I had no idea how you got to that point. Discovering your wounds helped me to heal mine. And for that, I can't thank you enough.'

In the corner of Topaz's kitchen, was a large box with items wrapped in paper.

'I have something else for each of you, too: something that comes from my heart.'

One at a time, she handed them another gift. Annie was the first to open hers. Inside she found a portrait of her, Zac, and their dog, Max, running by the river. 'This is amazing! How did you do this? How did you paint thi without us sitting down for you?'

'This...I painted this from my heart,' she smiled, touching Annie's hand.

'This is for you, Kate,' Topaz said, offering her a painting to unveil.

'Oh my. Oh *my!*' Kate was speechless. Topaz had captured her in the midst of an archaeological dig, examining the smallest piece of mosaic. It was rich, earthy and showed a depth of intensity that had Kate's eyes glued to it. Everyone looked at the paintings in awe.

Francesca opened hers to reveal a portrait of her, barefoot, by tall sunflowers, and the Sun streaming down on the river behind her. 'There are no words, Topaz. This is beyond art.'

After long hugs, Lia opened her gift. No-one could speak. Lia wanted to talk. She wanted to ask, 'How do you know what my little sister looked like?' but the words wouldn't leave her throat. Lia figured that the angelic figure hovering over her in the portrait meant that Topaz must have paid a visit to her family to see a photo. The "angel" of Lia's sister held her hands, prayer-like, over Lia as she wrote in a notebook at Sam's Café and Bookshop. Tears fell down Lia's face. She mouthed the words 'thank you', but it was impossible for sound to follow them.

Topaz looked around the room. Everyone was crying. There were old, old hurts washing themselves away, laying themselves bare upon her wooden kitchen table. And it was okay. It was okay to cry.

Saph's portrait was of her playing cello, with children at her feet. 'Oh Sis, you've never painted anything for me before! Ever!' she laughed. 'This is fabulous. Thank you so much.'

'Róisín, my dear, dear friend. This is for you.' Topaz could feel the breath of everyone in the room almost stop. Róisín saw herself, thirty-years younger, hand in hand with her husband, walking through a flower meadow in Ireland. And at the bottom of the painting were the words 'love never dies'. Thousands of starlings were in flight. Connor had obviously described every detail of the day his father died.

Róisín let her tears flow freely, and gently grabbed Topaz's hand. There was no need for words. They would come later.

Topaz turned to Camira. 'And you've shown me that life goes on.' Camira's portrait was of her naked in the birthing pool, just after birth, with Lavender in her arms, against the breast. The smile on her face was radiant, and her joy contagious. Loose, damp hair hung around her shoulders, and around her neck she wore a blessingway necklace. The water in the pool reflected the large red lilies in the bedroom, and the sanctity of Lavender's birth was forever captured in the painting.

She looked at the baby asleep in her sling, and said, 'That almost feels like a lifetime ago. So much has happened since then, hasn't it? That night truly was beautiful. Thank you so much for capturing Lavender's birth. It's amazing, truly amazing, to see her birth through your eyes. It's beautiful!'

'Now that you're all here, together, I was wondering if you'd like to make this a regular feature in our lives? We could meet up once a month, just us women, and the baby, of course, and continue to share and grow with each other.'

'Of course we would,' the women agreed. It was arranged that they'd meet on each New Moon, armed with good food, and take time to draw, write, dance, walk in the woods or just sit by the fire and chat. 'I've come to realise that every woman needs a circle of sisters. I'm so glad that I've found you all,' Topaz confided.

Epilogue

Five years later

Love and Loss

Connor is in the garden with our four-year-old twins, Raphael and Lisel. My heart is almost bursting with happiness. Every day I pinch myself. Is this real? Is this my life? Is Connor my husband? Did I *really* give birth by the fireside to those gorgeous children?

A Strauss waltz plays on the stereo, and I can't help but twirl around our home, and I allow myself the pleasure for a few minutes before continuing to water the house plants.

Our delightful children are kicking the ball between the trees, flicking up leaves of gold, aubergine, rust, ginger, mustard and burgundy. Summer has gone, and the nights are cool here in Cumbria. Their giggles keep us warm. As we settle into Autumn, I give thanks for another year of my life. Another year with people who see the best in me, and want the best for me. Another year with people who love me.

I've learnt as much from life through softness, tenderness and love as through any of the hard knocks, traumas and tragedies that I've endured.

Mosaic went on to win many awards, and we've since worked on two other books together. Connor sold The Children's Labyrinth without regret, and together we've created our simple, yet meaningful, life.

At every New Moon, I meet with my *Does Life Begin at 40?* women's circle, with the welcome addition of Sapphire and Camira. We celebrate life, and each other, with laughter, good food and creativity.

Róisín has become one of my most dear friends, proving that girlfriends don't need to be from the same generation. She's apprenticing Camira in the art of shamanic midwifery. Camira is a natural with women and babies, and has such a nurturing heart. I love her dearly.

We took a leaf out of Annie's book and have chosen to homeschool our children. It wasn't a hard choice. Connor and I have chosen freedom in our working lifestyle. It made sense to offer the same to our children.

Zac often comes by this way with his dog, and takes the children for a walk down the road and in the woods.

Our days have a gentle rhythm. Connor writes for a few hours each morning, while I'm with the children. We share the middle of the day together as a family, taking walks, playing, going on picnics; and in the afternoon, the children have dad time or dad-and-grandmother time while I work on my art. Róisín has enjoyed these last few years with her grandchildren enormously, and it has brought untold healing.

I'm not sure how I would have survived mothering twins without her and Connor. Róisín was always there, unobtrusively, in her quiet manner. I felt like I spent the few first years of the twins' lives glued to a sofa or bed breastfeeding, but I was nurtured like a queen.

They still return to the breast from time to time, usually when they've scraped a knee, or at bedtime when they're overtired. To see them outside now, playing, laughing ~ a vision of health and vibrancy ~ is proof of mother-love, father-love, grandparent-love and the love of a gaggle of biological and surrogate aunties and uncles. They're blessed to have my father living nearby with Saph and Jeff. A grandmother and a grandfather, from either side of the family tree, to dote on them, and nurture and love them.

If you're thinking my rural idyll is a bit too saccharine, I'll tell you this: These ordinary days are like natural medicine. I wouldn't have it any other way. These days heal wounds that are deep and painful.

My sister, my beautiful sister, Saph, endured three miscarriages. Two of them were in the second trimester. The grief was heavy and deadlier than thick pollution. Family is what helped her through. It's what helped all of us through. When you love someone, their pain is your pain.

Her third pregnancy ended at five months. Our parents were driving up from the south to offer support when they were involved in a head-on crash in torrential rain. My mother was killed instantly. There are times in life when you wonder if it is possible to move forward. Will the Sun ever rise above the horizon again?

I might be enjoying what others consider a perfect life but all I can say is: *let me enjoy it.* Let me hold on to every beautiful, ordinary second, because each one of them is extraordinary. I've learned rituals of the heart, and that every day is sacred, no matter what it brings our way. Connor and I protect our family life, and we nurture the family bond through meaningful daily acts.

Róisín initiated us into the sacred and ancient art of organic burial, as is the province of shamanic midwifery. Standing by our side, Róisín guided Sapphire and I as we tended our mother's body here, at home. We washed and bathed her in herbal water and essential oils, and brushed her hair. Her body was wrapped in linen winding cloths, and we laid her to rest in the woodland behind our home. She was as beautiful in death as in life. I feel blessed to have seen her this way, rather than preserved with formaldehyde, and her body handled by strangers in a morgue. Here, she was with loved ones.

Róisín officiated the ceremony, just as she had at our wedding, which was such a beautiful day: Connor and I, barefoot under the cherry trees, declaring our love before friends and family; Sapphire playing Schubert's Serenade on cello.

Watching my father, Connor and Jeff gently lower my mother down into the earth was an experience that I find hard to describe. Yes, it was an ending, and a painful one at that, but it was also a beginning. I could see that. Her shrouded body was now in sacred ground: with Mother Earth, the archetypal mother; and I found great comfort in that. I thought back to Camira's blessingway and about my long line of ancestresses. I was desperately sad that Mother would no longer be with us, or to watch the grandchildren she loved so very much, or that she'd ever meet Saph's children.

Róisín taught me so much about life and death. She taught all of us. *Midwives were the original undertakers*, she said. Their job was to bring people into the world, and to prepare them for burial when they departed. I've been conscious not to project my need for a mother onto her. She's my friend, and that comes before anything. But oh, what a *great* grandmother she is to our children.

Sapphire's grief for her third lost baby was shadowed greatly by our mother's death, and our need to provide support for Dad. These were long, painful days for him. The love of his life: *gone*. And yet, in many ways we all felt even closer to Mum. We felt her presence. Sometimes it was in a song or a scent in the air that couldn't be explained. More than once we thought we heard her voice. It is true to say that we all felt her around us: That she had walked through a curtain to the other side, but she hadn't truly gone.

Sapphire ended up applying for a post as a music therapist in the local orphanage. She loved teaching cello, and found it hard to give up her practice after so many years, but deep within she knew she had to give of herself in a way that was so profound it would break the shell that was forming around her achingly heavy heart.

Her daughter, Hope, is six months old now and thriving. Róisín had done a lot of dream therapy with Saph, which seemed to make a huge difference.

Life isn't perfect, but I've discovered that when you have love in your life, whether it's from a lover, a sister or a friend, that love is a cushion. Family is at the centre of life's meaning, and I've come to understand that all the worldly success and material gain doesn't provide the nurturing that so many people seek.

I was once told that the man I was looking for in my heart was also looking for me. We found each other. Every day I give thanks. I came to realise that I avoided relationships after Andy *not* because I was afraid to love, but because I had so very much love to give. It was only with hindsight that I recognised that I had honoured myself enough to know that I hadn't met anyone worthy of fully committing to. Until Connor. He's always making me laugh, even when I've had a bad day or we have trauma in our lives; he can still make me smile. I've often wondered if he's even human, or just a figment of my imagination. And then I see him playing rough and tumble with our children, and hear them all laughing out loud, and I know: I know with all my heart that he's real. We're real. Love's real. It's not true that you don't know what you've got until it's gone. We *all* know what we have in our lives. The truth is that many people don't appreciate what they've got until it's gone. Lia taught me that. She said that the grass is always greener where we water it.

When I hear Connor in the shower each morning singing opera, I smile. When he massages my back by the fire at night with jasmine essential oil and coconut oil, just like he did through my pregnancy, I give thanks.

At night, he reads Rumi or Kahlil Gibran to me. I know that I have found a love that transcends one lifetime. I'll always be grateful that Connor found me, and that he waited so patiently for me, yet I know in my heart that that could never have happened unless I'd found myself first. When we spent our first day together, Connor sang *If tomorrow never comes, would she know how much I loved her...* Some might think it was premature to sing a song like that at the start of our relationship, but as Connor says, he loved me from the first time he saw my photo. He says 'he remembered me from another time'... I believe him.

I've learnt what human love is really all about. We know what it means to love unconditionally. It's encoded in our soul. We've come to Earth to experience human love in all its forms and imperfections. Human love can be messy, and it can hurt. We are here to be human. I know that, now. Relationships are a reflection of our self-worth. I changed my life around by waking up each morning thankful for the day, thankful for this life. If tomorrow never comes, I *will* always know how much he loved me. He has never left me in any doubt.

*And we all lived
happily ever after.*

176

With gratitude

To Sara Simon for the beautiful cover illustration. You are brilliant! Thank you. I truly hope we work together on many more books.

Thank you to my songbird, Mandy Bingham, for singing into my pre-dawn writing life each morning. It was just you, me and the birds up early, syster!

To Sara, Eliza, Paul and Kathryn for taking the time to read through the raw manuscript ~ and for your feedback. Writing your first novel is like learning to walk. You need people around to cheer you on!

Thank you to my beloved, Paul, for always holding me together.

Thank you to the women in my circle of friendship, whether near or far. I'm grateful for you.

About the author

Veronika Robinson is married to the love of her life, Paul, and together they have two inspiring home-educated teenage daughters. They live in an old farmhouse in the beautiful Eden Valley, Cumbria, and together they edit an international magazine on parenting.

Veronika is never happier than when her hands are in the dark, moist soil and there's warm sunshine on her skin. Other passions include psychological astrology, cello music, reading and writing, gardening by the Moon, long chats on the phone with friends, cooking up a storm in the kitchen with her daughters, and walking hand-in-hand with her husband.

Veronika spent her teenage years reading Mills and Boon romance novels while she was supposed to be studying text books on how to dissect frogs and other ghastly things, like maths.

She believes in love at first sight, and is a hopeless romantic.

To keep up to date with her writing projects, visit:
www.veronikarobinson.com
Her daughter, Eliza, is also a novelist.
See: www.elizaserenarobinson.com

About the artist

Sara Simon is a lifelong artist whose creativity was encouraged from an early age, and who rarely goes anywhere without a sketchbook and pencil. After Art College, she detoured, in the Nineties, via a degree and employment in graphic design, but returned to paint and paper after becoming a mother and rejoining what she considers her true creative path. Today her arts include painting, drawing, writing, sewing, baking and too many other expressions to list.

Inspired by the outdoors, other people and the experiences of life, she's also devoted to gentle living and conscious parenting. Sara works from home in the Peak District, UK, where she lives with her husband and two sons. This is her third collaboration with Veronika. She illustrated *The Mystic Cookfire: the sacred art of creating food to nurture friends and family* and *Baby Names Inspired by Mother Nature*.

Visit www.sarasimon.co.uk

Lightning Source UK Ltd.
Milton Keynes UK
UKOW051218150413

209235UK00007B/119/P